I0535447

J. J. Houston

Murder on Moon Street
by

B·K· CRAWFORD

Edited by Mandy Cummins

Published in the United States of America
Mind Key Publishing ©2015 **Second Edition** @2016
All Rights Reserved

Mind Key Publishing

ISBN: 978-0-9912936-0-5

This book is dedicated to the adventures of childhood and to each member of my family—those brave, brave souls whose love surrounds and sustains me.

Table of Contents

Prologue
June 7, 1963

The state trooper knelt on one
knee and pressed his face so close to mine I could
smell the hotdog he ate for lunch—mustard and
relish. My nose wrinkled in protest. He stared,
trying to read the road maps in my eyes while I
gawked at the massive craters in his face. I didn't
like his voice, it rang deep and loud and with him
so close to begin with, I didn't understand his
need to shout. Okay, maybe I did, but I'm not
deaf. His goofy gray hat leaned so far over his
brow I wondered how he could see, and the strap
cut under his chin so that when he moved his jaw
to speak, the hat jiggled on his head. I found that
kind of funny, but nothing else about the
situation comforted me in any way. The strong
cologne, the loud voice, his chest full of badges
and pins, the starched uniform, and the
handcuffs hanging off his belt—I thought I might
leave a puddle on Momma's stuffed chair. I
might have felt differently if I thought this fella
believed me, but I could see he didn't. He kept
leaning in closer and I felt the urge to plant the
heel of my foot on his nose just to create some
distance and teach him some manners, but then I
thought maybe I ought not. He asked the same

B.K. Crawford

questions over and over, but worded them differently—adults think they can catch you in a lie that way. He shook his head when my story stayed the same; he just didn't want to buy a dime of it. His partner stood staring out the window at Lord knows what, with the palm of his hand resting on the butt of his pistol. Now and again he would turn to shake his head like I was the saddest liar this side of Washington, D.C. My Daddy hovered in the doorway, hands on his hips, his branding glare ripping me from one end to the other, and I wondered if he would let those dopey cops lock me in a cage for the rest of my life. Only Momma seemed to believe a stitch of my story and Lord if she didn't look unsure during the questioning. I didn't care. Those jokers could have asked me every question under the sun and it wouldn't have changed the truth. I figured when they were done with me, they would go ask Joey and he would tell them the same thing I told them. Then they would go see for themselves and they would choke and gag and wish to God they never got out of bed.

B.K. Crawford

That Girl Hatin' Bug
ВЖВ

Two days ago, I stood on the top bunk staring at my calendar with a goofy grin pasted over my face. Saturday, June 5th, it said, right there in bold.

Climbing down the ladder, I inspected my room one more time. I'd done a pretty good job of it, as long as no one opened the closet door. But, I always had something hiding under the bed I couldn't see without a flashlight. I wondered where I'd left my flashlight and thought, God help me if it's in the closet. But, wait... I used it last to nab night-crawlers for Daddy. I bet I left it in the mud room. I knew there were stairs under my feet, but I seemed to glide over them as I flew down the staircase and zoomed back up with the flashlight in hand.

Just as I suspected, three pair of panties and an old doll collected dust under the bed springs. I snatched them, stuffed the panties in the hamper, and hid the doll in a dresser drawer, cobwebs and all.

June 5th it said, right there in bold.

B.K. Crawford

My room looked as good as it ever has. Feeling lucky, I took the darts hanging around the edges of my dartboard and jammed them into the bulls-eye.

Just then, my mother yelled, "Get down here, Gerty, and wash these dishes."

Don't get the wrong idea, my name isn't Gerty, Gertrude, Matilda, or Miss Priss, those are just names my mother pulls out of her bag when she wants to get my attention. I ignored her...for the moment. See, I've known Momma for twelve years and I knew she had at least three more names lined up. I wouldn't have to worry until she screamed, '*Jennifer Jane Houston*.' That's when all hell breaks loose. Sometimes, though, she gets busy by the second or third time and forgets she wanted me to do something for her. Or, if I'm really lucky, she gives up and does the chores herself. Either way, I knew I had a few more minutes to get ready.

The room looked good, so I focused on my appearance. Standing in front of the dresser, I winced. The day may come when my freckles pack up their things and head out, but it won't happen anytime soon. It's awful having a face that looks like it got splashed by an erupting mud puddle. I might just be the

B.K. Crawford

ugliest toad in the pond. My hair is all wiry, not blonde, but not quite brown either, just a murky shade of yuck. I spit into the palms of my hands and tried to tame it a little, but no one has ever calmed a bull with a branding iron. So, I did what I always do, grabbed a hair band and tied it up.

It said June 5th, right there in bold.

I could have burst right out of my seams.

There ain't much traffic out here in the country—it's so quiet you can hear a field mouse fart—so I'd know when Aunt Celia and Uncle Joe arrived, but it wasn't them I ached to see, I wanted to see my cousin, Joey. They planned to drop him off and let him stay here a whole month while they went to take care of some business in Ohio. What kind of business? Didn't know, didn't care. I only cared about hanging with Joey. We're about the same age, me and him, but he's a few months older. Here's the thing, though, there ain't a boy in this whole world who can get into as much trouble as Joey and then slide out of it smooth as an otter on Grease River. Adults take his word for everything; it's almost like he spits voodoo dust every time he opens his mouth and dang if it doesn't put those grown-ups under a spell

B.K. Crawford

they can't seem to escape. It's really something to see. The other thing is, I've got an army of cousins, but most of them already went through the change that makes boys hate girls.

I thought I'd turn inside out waiting to hear car doors slam.

Turns out Aunt Celia and Uncle Joe had a flat on their way over here, so they didn't show up until after dinner. By that time, I'd eaten every fingernail and most of my toenails, too. I wish I could say the worrying stopped when they finally got here, but I won't lie.

Momma offered a late dinner to the lot of them, but Aunt Celia and Uncle Joe said they were already behind schedule because of the flat tire and if they didn't hit the road right away, they might as well not go at all. Any blind fool could see Aunt Celia didn't want to go anyway and my stomach twisted because if they didn't go to Ohio, then Joey wouldn't get to stay.

The adults inched their way toward the door, in a hurry to get the goodbyes said, and that's when the worst thing that could possibly happen pooped all over my world. Every time I tried to get Joey's attention, he'd

B.K. Crawford

turn his head away or drop his chin. I couldn't have tried any harder to get that boy to look at me, but he just wouldn't have an inch of it. Well, I thought I might as well up and die right there because anyone could see he'd been bitten by that girl-hatin' bug. Now, I need to know, what good is a day, a week, or a month in the company of a boy who hates girls?

So, there I sat on my lumpy mattress chewing my fingers down to the knuckles, crying so hard it's a wonder God didn't slam his door just so He could get some sleep. Joey snored on the lower bunk, oblivious. To think I spent the last two weeks staring at a calendar and chasing bugs out of my room for nothing.

B.K. Crawford

A Beautiful Wreck

ВЖВ

   Imagine my surprise in the morning when Joey admitted his guy pals ribbed him about going out to the country to play with his *girlfriend*. Like it was *my* fault. I hoped he'd get smarter as he grew older, because right then he seemed about as bright as a molasses turd.

   Joey glared like he might reach out and pop me one. I felt my lower lip start to tremble, but I put a stop to that by sucking it between my teeth. I already did all the crying I meant to do. I could have planted that boy six feet under without giving a dang how many weeds grew on top of him twenty years from now. He's not that much bigger than me and, as long as he didn't expect it, I probably could've hit him hard enough to make him see stars. Thing is, I had better things to do.

   See, the two of us made a truly awesome discovery last summer. But, because Joey had to go home, we didn't have nearly enough time to explore as we wanted. So, we made a pact. He made me solemnly swear I wouldn't go anywhere near our newly

B.K. Crawford

discovered treasure until he came back,
saying it could be very dangerous for me to
go alone. He didn't have to say so, I could
see it for myself. But here's the rub, I'm a
complete sucker for curious things. So,
keeping our pact was like asking me to sit still
while a scorpion knit a pair of booties in my
sock. I thought about that place every
minute of every day, all year long, but I kept
my word.

My face burned hot and my hands began
to tremble. I could've turned that boy inside
out and used him to paint my room red.

The memory of our time swimming at
Moon Mist Lake, the tobogganing, the
campfires, and the ice-skating, all of our
adventures and escapades over the years,
kept me grounded. Joey had no call to get
mad at me for something someone else did,
but I wouldn't join him in acting like an idiot.
If he wanted to spend the summer on his
own, so be it. As far as I could tell, our pact
had ended. I spent the morning getting
ready to go explore and I intended to do it,
with or without Joey.

He stared at me with laser beam eyes,
trying to burn holes through my skin as I
went to grab a can of oil off the porch to

B.K. Crawford

grease my bike chain. When I finished, I jerked the handlebars, swung the bike around, mounted up, and shoved off. Joey's hellfire glare followed me as I rode past. I flipped him a nasty toot-a-loo once I'd moved out of reach.

I listened to the grind and crunch of the dirt and gravel beneath my bike tires. Okay, so I cried a little, but the further I went the better I felt.

Moon Street has never been paved and she's got her ruts and potholes, especially after a hard rain. We're surrounded by farmland out here and the tractors, combines, and trucks with their big, heavy wheels don't do the road any favors. Believe me when I say Mr. Flint's cows don't make the best air freshener either, especially on a hot day. Thankfully, the breeze blew cool despite a bright sun. I enjoyed watching the light twinkle between the trees while I rode past, playing peek-a-boo with Mother Nature.

Glancing over my shoulder, I checked to see if Joey had followed. Nope. Even if he did want to come along, he'd have to ask my mother for the key to the storage shed in order to dig his bike out. That would take a

B.K. Crawford

bite out of the clock because Daddy buried everything behind the lawn mower and tiller last fall. If Joey had acted like anything but a total gopher hole, I would have helped him with the bike.

I caught a whiff of fresh-cut grass as I approached the Flint farm. The missus wore a billowy summer dress and high heels as she buzzed around the lawn on her fancy riding mower. Daddy says it's important to wear the right clothes for the right job and if one of Mrs. Flint's dresses ever gets caught in the wheel of her rider, she's in for one heck of a how-do-you-do. I suspect he's right. She raised a gloved hand and waved as I passed by. The minute I let go of the handlebar to wave back, my front tire sank into a rut and almost sent me skidding. Mrs. Flint saw this and shook her head like I was the dumbest invention since Silly Putty. Steadying the bike, I promised myself I'd pay a little more attention to the road ahead.

The road stretches about a mile and a quarter between my house and where it splits off. I wouldn't be going all the way to the end because my search would lead me to a small foot path on the left, not too far from my house.

B.K. Crawford

I'd ridden down Moon Street a million times and never noticed a path until last summer when I thought I saw something shiny sparkling through the trees. I dropped my bike and told Joey I wanted to go into the brush to see if I could find it and he followed along. That's when we found our hidden treasure.

Just thinking about it put a little more pep in my step, as Daddy likes to say, and I started pedaling faster until I realized I might miss the path if I moved too fast. So, I slowed down and focused on the brush growing around the tree line, careful not to put my bike in the ditch and mindful of the road ahead. Now and again, I checked for signs of Joey coming from behind, but no.

I can't imagine how I missed the path, but I did. I'd gone way too far and found myself just around the bend from the end of the road. I had to turn around and try again. Hopping off the bike, I flipped it around. There's already enough of my blood and skin mixed in the road gravel for me to know my bike is way too big to take a sharp turn.

See, while my Daddy is a genius with a wrench and a can of paint, he ain't got any money to burn because his small engine

B.K. Crawford

repair business is usually slow, so most of my things come from secondhand shops or the local dump. Like me, my bike will never win an award for being pretty, but it gets me where I want to go.

An hour went by while I rode up and down the road looking for the path and I was fit to be tied on two accounts. First, I couldn't find the path. Second, because of the argument with Joey, I forgot to bring my field bag and it had my lunch in it.

Mrs. Flint snoozed on her porch. She'd watched me ride by her house so many times, I'm sure I must have hypnotized her.

My frustration built and I imagined smoke spewing out of my ears, like Elmer Fudd chasing that waskly wabbit. I thought my legs might detach and walk on home without me, they felt so tired. So, I stopped and rested a bit. While I caught my breath, a tiny chipmunk scampered across the road and stopped to have a look at me, his cheeks filled to the brim with acorns or walnuts. He stood on his hind legs, twitched his nose, and tried to smile but his mouth was full of nuts. He looked so cute I wanted to snatch him up, give him a name, and take him home to live with me. He must've caught wind of my

B.K. Crawford

thoughts because he skittered off into the brush. I watched until his tail disappeared and—wouldn't you know it?—he found the path.

Well, to heck with tired. I dragged my bike into the brush and tried to wrestle it through, but the trees had grown so close together and the brush so thick, I didn't stand a chance. So, I propped the bike against a tree and took off on foot. Suddenly, everything went dark and I could barely keep track of the path, the sun not in such a cheery mood after all, so I crouched down until I found it easier to see, my heart pounding so hard you'd think the repo man had come a'knocking.

Finally, finally, finally—I had arrived. My triumph short-lived, I stopped when I heard a strange noise; hard to make out at first, but the closer I got, the more I realized—it sounded like that old house had the flu and was puking its guts out. That couldn't be. I navigated the brush like a skilled tight end, (Daddy taught me a lot about football over the years and even though I might rather watch a movie, my attitude is, if ya can't beat 'em, join 'em).

B.K. Crawford

Once I stood in front of my treasure, I took it all in. What a beautiful wreck. Half the roof had gone missing, you could see through the walls in most places, and the stone foundation had more cracks than a plumber's convention. It was *huge*. The best part? It still had furniture and stuff in it. Last year, we found money on a kitchen counter. Not a lot, but it's the thrill of the hunt, you know? I reached for the door knob, ready to twist, when I heard the puking noise again. It sounded so real, I froze. I heard it again and this time coughing and a low moan followed. I knew that moan. I swung the door open and there he stood, doubled over the kitchen sink, retching his guts out—King Donkey Butt. Joey.

Startled, he turned and motioned for me to go back. He didn't look angry anymore. Instead, the expression on his face sent a chill down my spine. Fear. I'd never seen Joey afraid before. He kept waving at me and I knew what he wanted, 'Get out,' is what that gesture meant, but I couldn't leave him standing there sick and scared. Besides, Joey would put on an act just so he could keep our glorious house all to himself. Somehow I knew it wasn't an act, though, and I began to

B.K. Crawford

absorb his fear. Rushing into the kitchen, I grabbed a rotting towel and wiped Joey's face with it. The scary thing? He let me. Then, I helped him into a chair, the only one in the room with four legs still attached. The smell of vomit hung so thick, I thought it a very lucky thing I forgot my lunch. I let him sit for a few minutes and then coaxed him out the door, away from the house, so he could breathe without sucking in his own puke fumes. The sun stopped pouting and I could see the snot on Joey's face, the gray color of his skin, the shaking, and the tears. What had done this to him?

"Did you eat a bad bean, or what?" I wanted to know.

He wouldn't look at me. "I ain't sick," he said, his voice mousy and small.

"You look sick as a dog."

He looked up at me but didn't say anything for a long time, his eyes studying my face, the wheels turning in his head. "You're gonna look sick, too," he finally said.

"Me? Why?"

"Because I know you, and I know you won't leave here until you see what I just saw." He choked out his words and then

B.K. Crawford

broke out crying. He-man, chew nails and shit bricks Joey, wailing like a little girl.

I didn't know what to think, but I did know this—something in the world had turned upside down and inside out.

B.K. Crawford

Shadows Of A Tattered Crucifix

ВЖВ

My mother made my favorite meal for dinner, macaroni and cheese with hamburger. Me and Joey didn't get much of it down, we just sort of pretended to eat— shoved a lot of it under our plates and fed the rest to Crusher, our ferocious pit bull who will climb a tree and whimper whenever he's attacked by a curious butterfly.

Getting through dinner without puking on my plate proved no small thing. Every now and then I had to pretend to have something in my eye so I could wipe away tears insisting on a prison break. Daddy almost caught on and asked why my hands were shaking. I had to think quick. I said I felt excited to have Joey over. Joey nodded and tried to smile, but it came out looking like something from the hall of mirrors at an amusement park. I guess it worked, though, Daddy just nodded and shrugged it off.

Momma told me to wash the dishes, so she never saw all the macaroni and cheese planted under our plates and Crusher went to bed good and full. For the first time I can ever remember, I couldn't wait for Daddy to

B.K. Crawford

tell us to go to bed. But, dang it all to Timbuktu, he got caught up in a movie with some goofy detective and we weren't shooed off until an hour past our bedtime.

I let Joey have the top bunk. We usually draw straws for it, but my stomach hadn't finished doing cartwheels and I couldn't see how being up there would make it any better. I don't know if Joey felt the same way, but he hadn't climbed the ladder yet. We waited until the house went dark and quiet and then waited some more because the walls are thin. Once Joey decided it safe to talk, he started whispering.

"I told you not to look." He said, like rubbing it in could change what already happened.

"Too late now," I said, thinking it wasn't just what I saw that upset me, but how awful it smelled. God almighty. A stench like that can make puke seem like an expensive perfume. I still gag when I think about it.

"We better tell someone tomorrow," Joey said, but I couldn't tell if he meant it or not. Only a small trickle of moonlight streamed through the window but I could see Joey still retching, like he might throw up on the floor. No way I'd clean it up if he did.

B.K. Crawford

"I'll be right back," I said, and made a quick trip to the bathroom. I came back and handed him a little soap angel that smelled like lavender. It's one of Momma's prized possessions, part of a set that's been collecting dust in the bathroom for a couple years. I'd put it back before she could notice it missing. Joey looked at me like I'd lost my last marble, like he didn't think a fake angel could do him any good at all.

I gave my eyes a roll and pointed at the soap, "Hold it under your nose for a few minutes, it'll erase the memory."

"Oh," is all he said and gave it a good, long sniff. I knew it worked right away because his shoulders dropped and he smiled for the first time since we got back home.

"How long do you suppose it's been there?" I asked, and he knew I didn't mean the soap. "Do you think it was there last year when we found the place?" My skin crawled at the thought.

"Hell if I know." He shrugged and breathed in that angel some more.

"Think about it," I hissed, careful to keep my whisper real low. "It wouldn't smell so bad if it's been there for years, but it would

B.K. Crawford

look a whole lot better if it's only been there a week. Right?"

He inhaled the angel so hard it's a wonder he didn't suck her right up a nostril.

"You're a freakin' genius," he said. "Now we know it's been there somewhere between a week and a hundred years. Brilliant."

That's gratitude for you. I wanted to snatch that angel out of his hands and shove it right up his backside.

"I don't think we should tell anybody yet," I said and kept talking because I knew he would argue. "If we tell, then the place will be swarming for a couple days, but then it'll be all over and we'll never know who did it, or what really happened."

Joey handed the soap back to me and started to climb the ladder. "J.J., I don't care who did it, or what really happened."

Who knows why, but that just made my blood boil. I sniffed that angel until it didn't have any lavender left in it, then took it back to the bathroom. By the time I got back to my room, which wasn't more than a minute, Joey was either asleep or faking it. Either way, he'd finished talking. I'd have to convince him to keep his mouth shut later.

B.K. Crawford

I tried to sleep, but what I saw that day played over and over again inside my head.

Joey kept telling me not to go back into the house, but I wouldn't listen. Part of me knew I shouldn't go in because I could see something had seriously upset Joey, but the other part just plain didn't believe him. It's a mean trick, the way we don't want to believe what someone else says until we see for ourselves. I marched right into the living room—careful to step around the holes in the floor boards—and searched for a trap door. I found it tucked in a dark corner where I never would have noticed if Joey didn't tell me where to look. It felt heavy, but I managed to yank it up. I looked down into the black hole in the floor and wished I had a flashlight, but I'd left that in my field bag with my lunch. I could smell it then, but just a faint stink, like when a mouse dies inside a wall. I tried to pull my shirt collar over my nose but it wouldn't stay. I stood there staring into the hole for a couple minutes, not really wanting to go down the stairs by myself. The boards were older than the hills—what if one of the stairs broke and dumped me into the hole? Joey yelled for me to come back out, so I figured if I wanted

B.K. Crawford

to see what he saw, I best do it quick. I gathered my courage and took the first two stairs real slow. Then I realized the longer I stood on the stairs, the more stress I put on them, so I practically flew down the rest.

The basement only had two small windows and they were caked with grime, so I couldn't see any better than if I were staring at the bottom of Momma's cast iron frying pan. I stood still for a minute while my eyes adjusted, even then, I couldn't see but a few feet ahead. I noticed the smell getting stronger and if I had half a brain, I would've turned around right then, but curiosity has killed my cat so many times it's living on borrowed tuna.

The dirt floor smelled old and musty and the stones in the foundation walls oozed a sweaty slime. I swatted at my head as I moved forward because I could feel cobwebs getting stuck in my hair. My legs became suddenly reluctant, like they belonged to a stiff-kneed plastic doll rather than a real human being. I forced myself to keep going.

The basement held a few recognizable things, things you'd expect to find in an old house, like mason jars collecting dust on tilted shelves, boxes of old clothes, a coal

B.K. Crawford

shovel, bits of tangled rope, splintered wooden crates, empty oil cans, and rusted tools. The offending odor grew a lot stronger and I felt my stomach retch. I almost turned back.

That's when I saw it, hanging on the far wall like the shadow of a tattered crucifix. Covering my nose with my hands, I moved close enough to see the decomposed body of a young boy chained to the wall, still wearing his cowboy outfit, dusty, frayed, and full of holes, one cowboy boot still attached, the other standing upright on the ground beneath his dangling leg. The bones on his left cheek were shattered, leaving a hole, like someone had clocked him good. I could feel a scream broiling in the acid churning in my throat. I don't know what I expected, a dead dog maybe, or a mutilated calf, but not this. My instinct said to run, but I couldn't move. I just stood there staring, waiting for the vomit. Then I watched in mortal horror as the cowboy hat slowly lifted up, exposing the skeleton's empty eye sockets. I tried to imagine what might cause the hat to rise like that when a rat burst out of the skull, hurling itself at me. Needless to say, I turned tail and

B.K. Crawford

ran, swearing never to return to that house, ever.

B.K. Crawford

The Last Inch Of A Burning Fuse
ВЖВ

  The next day, Daddy busied himself building hills for his red potatoes while Momma flipped through the Montgomery Ward catalog, pretending she had a chance to buy something nice. Another sunny, summer day. Joey and me loaded up our supplies and rode down to flat rock where we could talk in private.

  Flat rock is a massive boulder large enough to hold twenty people if you squeeze them in good and tight. I named the rock myself. It's not easy to climb but if you know where all the nooks and crannies are, you can get on top without cracking your head. The boulder sits just off the road about two miles from my house; we discovered it a few years back when we were looking for wild strawberry patches.

  I sat on the rock eating a handful of berries that grow at the base of the boulder while Joey stared off, looking at nothing in particular.

  "It's murder," he mumbled, then turned to me and spoke with conviction, "We have to tell."

B.K. Crawford

Murder on Moon Street

I wondered why he stared like it was me who killed that poor kid, but I decided not to take a swing at his bee's nest. I knew he hadn't gotten over his pals embarrassing him and he'd likely blame me for everything under the sun. I popped a big red strawberry in my mouth and bit down.

"I know it's murder, but like I said, if we tell, the cops will come and we won't be able to get anywhere near that house for weeks. Gotta be clues in there somewhere. The police will take the body away, stuff it in a box somewhere, slap a number on a file, and we'll never know what happened."

"We're not supposed to know what happened. We're kids. Even if we could find clues, we can't solve a real murder. We need to tell and we need to do it today."

"Joey, that house of horrors is so close to my place, we could spit on it from my window."

He lifted an eyebrow and looked at me like I'd gone nuts. "So?" He seemed aggravated with what he must have seen as the stupendousness of my stupidity.

"So, you said it yourself, we're kids. Somebody killed a kid, chained him to the wall, and left him there to rot. We have to

B.K. Crawford

care if the cops can't do this job right because we could be next."

I guess I didn't look so stupid as he first thought because the expression on his face changed from aggravation to startled fear as the lights went on. He practically flew off flat rock and stumbled in the tall grass on his way to his bike, which he'd parked in the ditch next to mine.

No doubt about it, Joey had made up his mind and nothing I could do or say would change it. I could tell by the way he didn't let up on his bike pedals—he meant to go home to have a chat with Daddy. I reckoned all hell would break loose. For one thing, Daddy would be a bug-eyed hornet when he realized we didn't tell him about the body when we first found it. I supposed Joey planned to put that blame on me and, even though it would piss me off to the moon and back, I knew the fault fell on me since I said we shouldn't tell. The way I saw it, Daddy would be so mad, I'd be lucky if I got television privileges again before someone invented a way to watch it in your sleep. What could I do about it, though? Done is done.

B.K. Crawford

Like I said, adults give their stamp of approval to Joey no matter what he says or how he says it. They never believe a word I say. I could say the world is round and glued together by earth worms and someone will tell me I'm wrong. Still, I've heard it said there's an exception to every rule. I suppose that means if the speed limit is fifty-five and a woman is having a baby in your car, it's okay to drive sixty-five. Maybe it means God is love when He ain't telling somebody or another to slay someone else. What it meant that day was Daddy laughed at Joey and didn't believe a word he said, and damn if it wasn't the *one* time Joey told the truth.

Daddy got up off his potato hills, brushed the dirt off his knees, stretched a little and turned to me.

"J.J.?" He said, and I bust out crying like a kid caught with a bag of Tootsie Rolls stuffed in her hat.

Then he looked at us like he might be taking Joey's story a bit more serious.

Momma must've heard me bawling because she came running out on the porch and yelled at Daddy, "What did you *do*?"

B.K. Crawford

"Not a goddamn thing," Daddy growled, like he might bite Momma's head off if she said another word, but that didn't stop her.

"Then why is J.J. puking in her shoes?" She hollered.

I didn't realize she'd seen me do that, but sure enough.

Daddy's face turned beet red and he looked madder than a catfish chewing on an empty hook. He took ten steps toward Momma, so close she knew she better not say another word, then he pointed at Joey and me. "They said they found a body in the old Hornbrook house. Somebody's about to get a whoopin' for lying."

I blew more chunks in the grass, Daddy had his belt undone, and Joey looked ready to turn tail when Momma said, "Cripes, Denny. What if they did?"

Daddy let go of his belt, grabbed my shoulder in one hand and Joey's in the other, dragged us to the porch, and slapped us down on the step.

"Go get my huntin' rifle," he barked at Momma.

"Don't you *dare*," She screamed, and I knew she thought the same thing I did. The

B.K. Crawford

last inch of Daddy's fuse had burnt away and he meant to murder all of us.

"Get it," he snarled and she knew she best do what he said.

While he waited for Momma, he grabbed us by the hair and jerked our faces up to meet his.

"Don't you lie to me," he bellowed, and we knew in our heart of hearts, one wrong word and we were worm food, "What did you find?"

"It's there, I swear," Joey coughed through his snot, "A little boy in a cowboy suit, chained to the wall. Smells to high heaven."

Daddy didn't expect that. I think he expected us to say how sorry we were for pulling his leg. His face went white and he stepped back, blinking like he couldn't believe what Joey just said. He pulled himself together, put his accusing face back on and said, "I'm about to call the police. If you're lying to me, you'll both rot in jail. Understood?"

"I'm not lying," Joey insisted.

"All right then," Daddy said, and stormed past us on his way into the house.

B.K. Crawford

Ain't That The Way?
ВЖВ

A dozen police cruisers kicked up dust on our little country lane and I'm sure the neighbors wondered why the cops were flying down Moon Street like it didn't have a rut in it. Lights flashing, sirens wailing, just like on Dragnet.

Ain't no garage or driveway at our house, so half the cruisers parked on the lawn, the other half in the hayfield next door. I've never seen so many people in uniform all at once, so many guns, so many men fired up and looking for a fight. Vietnam meets Mayberry RFD. I don't know what's more nerve-jittering, dead bodies, or live ones with guns.

The old fella in charge, Lt. Newman, sat me and Joey down and asked all kinds of questions, wrote everything down, and then asked the same questions over and over until he decided we were telling the truth.

It's an adult world. Once they got what they wanted from us, they told me and Joey to stay put with Momma while they headed out for the Hornbrook house. Ain't that the way? They left us out of the action and we

B.K. Crawford

were miffed, but Joey made a good point when he said he didn't want that smell in his nose again anyway.

Later, me and Joey were sent to bed early without dinner. I figured I'd be the first girl in the county to attend the senior prom at age eighty-two. I'd need one of those walkers with the tennis balls stuck to the legs and an oxygen machine.

Surprisingly, we weren't slapping metal cups against jailhouse bars, yelling at Deputy Doofus because he forgot to give us a phone call.

Once again, I felt fit to be tied, madder than a bull with a rubber band tied around its jewels. None of this would have happened if Joey listened to me in the first place and kept his mouth shut. But no. *Everybody* knows better than J.J. Houston.

Joey sniffled on the top bunk, a bag of ice dripping over his shiner. Wasn't Daddy who gave him that black eye and it wasn't a cop. I did it. It's not my fault Joey decided to tell Daddy what we found. I told him not to. It wasn't my fault the police showed up here. And it sure as heck wasn't my fault when they came back saying they didn't find a darned thing in the basement at the

Hornbrook house. But, being the donkey butt that he is, when we got in trouble for supposedly lying, Joey decided to take a swing at me out of frustration. It's not my fault I saw it coming, not my fault I'm faster than he is, and who knows whose fault it was when his eye smacked into my fist.

I paced my room until I'd walked twenty miles between the dresser and the bunk beds in the space of two hours. When I finally turned the light out and slipped under the covers, I wondered why someone would take that body out of the basement after leaving it there for so long, and right before the police showed up.

B.K. Crawford

Mermaid Hair

ВЖВ

Momma and Daddy let us have breakfast the following day and said we could go outside, but told us to stay in our own yard. Joey helped Daddy in the garden and I guess Momma tinkered around inside. I sat on my favorite stone beside the stream that flows behind our house. On a warmer day, I might have thought about taking a swim. My cousins and me used to swim here in our underwear when we were little. I'm too old to swim in just my undies now, but I don't mind the memories.

An emerald moss is attached to the rock bed at the bottom of the creek and it looks like long strands of mermaid hair swaying in the current. It's mighty pretty but makes for a slippery walk across the stream. The creek is fed by a spring running off the mountain, so the water runs cold no matter what time of year it is. Sometimes, that's just what you need on a hot summer day. I go to the stream a lot because I like the way the sun bounces off the stones, I like watching the tadpoles play, and I like having room to think.

B.K. Crawford

Daddy told me at the breakfast table to count myself lucky the cops didn't lock me up for making false reports to law enforcement officers. Well, you know I told him I didn't make up a darn thing. Then—me and my big mouth—I just had to say it wasn't my idea to call the cops and I would have been just as satisfied if Daddy had gone over to the Hornbrook house to check things out *before* he called the police. His face fanned out like a cobra and his eyes got real small, and just like you'd do if you were faced with such a mortal creature, I stayed perfectly still. Someday, I might learn to keep my trap shut, but I'm guessing it might not happen in this lifetime. Anyway, I put on my straightest face and told Daddy point-blank, I didn't lie. What'd he say? He said he knew I didn't lie because even though they didn't find a body, something sure stank that place up, plus he saw chain marks on the wall and holes in the mortar where the chain pins had been. I picked my jaw up off the floor and asked why he'd punished me, then. What'd he say? He said because I didn't tell him right away after we found the body and that's what they call a lie of omission. Saw that one coming, didn't I?

B.K. Crawford

I felt relieved to know Daddy believed me and it explained why he'd let us come outside; Daddy never would have let me out of my bedroom if he thought I'd lied to him. But he did forbid me and Joey to go anywhere near the Hornbrook house— dammit all to hell and back. I told him I didn't find that fair, especially since the body was gone. My Daddy's not dumb, though. He knew as well as I did we had a killer on the loose who seemed hungry for young blood. So, he told me one more time he'd tan my hide if I went anywhere near that place. Then he reminded me I still had work to do excavating the Briarhill caves. When he said that, it felt like he walked right into my head and flicked a light switch on. I still wonder how I could have forgotten about the caves.

See, I had it all figured out. I'd grow up, go off to college and become an archeologist so I could study prehistoric artifacts. Why? Because I gotta know who really made those pyramids in Egypt and how they did it. I want to know what happened to Atlantis, and I want to know what really happened to the Mayan civilization. I've read every book I could get my paws on and some I read two or three times because our school library

B.K. Crawford

doesn't have nearly enough to satisfy my curiosity. I think it's possible ancient people had technology we can only dream of today. Because of that, I've got a sneaking suspicion we're being lied to by historians, politicians, teachers, and pretty much everybody else. I'll have a long way to go to prove it, though.

A couple summers ago, I told Daddy about the books I read and what I thought about them. He took me by the hand and marched me up over Briarhill, which is on the other side of the road from our house. It's a big ol' hill and steep, perfect for sleds and toboggans, but hard to walk, so it took us over an hour to get to the place Daddy had in mind to show me. I could hardly believe it when I found myself standing at the base of a long line of caves carved into the side of the hill. Daddy brought flashlights and everything—turned out to be one of the best days of my life. If I had to guess, I'd say Daddy had fun, too, popping in and out of those caves and sifting through the dirt looking for treasure. He actually found a right nice Indian arrowhead he let me keep as a reminder of what you can find if you ain't afraid to get your hands dirty. After that day, he let me go on up there by myself, but

B.K. Crawford

warned me to be careful because mountain lions, bears, and rattlesnakes enjoy a good cave as much as anybody.

I tossed a small stone into the creek and watched the water swallow it. Dilemma. While exploring the caves is definitely exciting, finding out what happened to that poor little boy seemed just as important. When you stop to think about it, whoever killed that boy and moved his body wasn't but a stone's throw away on several occasions. It didn't seem a coincidence someone moved the body so soon after we found it. I had to decide, right then and there, what was most important. I didn't imagine Daddy would give me much choice in the matter, but like he always says, there's more than one way to pop a frog.

B.K. Crawford

Bear Slapped
ВЖВ

No way under the dripping sun would Daddy let me go anywhere that day, so I waited until the next morning to pack up my equipment—lunch, canteens, digging tools, and everything else I needed to look like I planned to excavate. I pulled the heavy field bag over my shoulder and asked Daddy if I could go. He looked me over real good, then nodded. I felt my stomach do a flip for joy and turned tail before Joey could ask if he could come along. Truth be told, he didn't ask and I didn't expect him to, besides which, I would have said no.

I trudged up the hill and stayed on my path until I'd gone clean out of sight. Then, I veered off course and took a sharp right to enter the Briarhill trail.   Ducking branches and hopping over fallen logs, I made my way south, all the while remembering what Daddy told me long ago, *'You never walk Briarhill trail on your own.'*

Unfortunately, I'd have to use the trail to skirt far enough around so Daddy wouldn't know I hadn't gone excavating, but actually meant to sneak off to the Duke farm to get

B.K. Crawford

Bo so we could go back to the Hornbrook
house together. I reckoned I'd stay on the
trail for about a mile and then work my way
back down to Moon Street. Along the way, I
found a birch branch I turned into the perfect
walking stick. For a moment, I became
Sacagawea, helping Lewis and Clark to
navigate the harrowing landscape.

   I'd gone about half a mile when I found
out why you never walk Briarhill trail on your
own.

   Squirming through the tight trees, I
marveled at Mother Nature's neat little
tricks—the earthy smell of dew on heather,
the different shapes created when moss
forms on the trees, and the funny way
mushrooms grow everywhere, even on rocks.
Lost in a blissful forest trance, I heard a God-
awful snap and felt my walking stick crack in
two. Startled, I looked down to see what had
eaten my beautiful birch stick. Bear trap. If
not for what happened next, I would've
counted myself lucky to still have two
working feet. Yes, I felt fortunate to have
avoided the bear trap, but luck is oil and I am
water. Not thirty feet ahead of me, rooting
through the fallen foliage, stood a young bear
cub. Small, black, cute as a button. My heart

B.K. Crawford

thumped against my chest. I'd never seen a bear so close, but I do listen when my Daddy talks so I knew I'd stepped neck deep in doo-doo.

'Where there's a cub, there's a momma,' he'd said. *'You don't mess with a momma bear, they are extremely protective of their young and they'll rip your head off just for breathing.'*

A bear, as I understand it, is the type of animal to ask questions *after* the waiter brings the check. I heard her rustling in the brush nearby and felt the desire to run like the devil, but, like I said, I pay attention to my Daddy and he said there ain't no way a human can outrun a bear. They might look too heavy to run fast, but think again. So, I slowly removed my field bag and set it out of the way. Then, quick as I could without making too much of a racket, I picked up some leaves and sticks and poked them into my hair. Then I sat down and covered myself with foliage. When the momma bear came into view, she stopped to scratch her back on a nearby tree. Forcing myself to stay still, I closed my eyes and pretended, with all my might, to be a tree.

B.K. Crawford

J. J. HOUSTON ©43
Murder on Moon Street

Lordy, my knots are itchy today and, drat, my branches aren't flexible enough to reach the itch, but—oh look— my acorns are budding nicely. Go the other way bear, I'm just a tree, soaking up the sun and spreading my roots so you'll have some nice shade to nap in. Go the other way, now, nothing to see here.

She sauntered over to her cub and gave it a nudge. I thanked Jesus the bear didn't look the least bit alarmed, which I thought would be so if she felt threatened by my presence. I continued to stretch my branches toward the sun and willed my leaves to grow, resisting the urge to shiver off the relentless bugs eating at my bark. Then my oily luck ran out. The bear suddenly lifted her nose to the wind and sharply turned her head toward me. Time ceased to exist, my bladder refused to hold, and the urge to run fired up every nerve in my body, but I knew if I so much as twitched, my goose was pâté.

Her growl sounded louder than a grunt of mild annoyance. When I heard her snarl I understood, the shallow gulps of air I took were the last breaths of my life. I wouldn't return to my house that night and my parents would call the state troopers back to

B.K. Crawford

do a wide sweep until they found my shattered bones lying where the bear burped them out. You would think knowing this would drive a person mad with quaking fear, but the thought actually had the opposite effect and soothed me in the strangest way. About to die, I knew how, where, and by what means, and it was okay. How much can it hurt after the first bite, right?

A frantic voice bellowed inside my head but I knew it didn't belong to me because I felt calm. The voice screamed at me the way Daddy screams when he catches me sipping his beer. *Run*, it demanded. Stupid voice. Whoever it belonged to didn't know jack about bears. I closed my eyes and very, very, slowly lowered my chin to my chest, becoming a dead tree. No more budding acorns, no more itchy bark, just a rotten timber waiting for the grace to fall. I could hear the bear coming closer but I refused to move. I kept my eyes closed, but I could tell from the rustle of leaves, she cautiously approached. Her gurgling grunts and growls told me just how close she'd come. She pressed her snout against my ear and sniffed. Still, I refused to move, dead trees don't move. She sniffed again and then she

B.K. Crawford

thumped me hard upside the head. I couldn't tell if she'd used a paw or snout, but I saw stars and fell over. Still, I didn't move. Three cheers for my drama coach, or maybe the bear just picked up the scent of the tuna fish in my field bag, but she moved away and started sniffing at the bag. I heard a frantic scuffle, then heard the bear trudging back the way she came. I sat petrified for several eternities and when I could hear nothing more, I opened my eyes. The bears were gone and they had taken my field bag with them.

I'd soiled myself, would have no lunch, and I'd need a doozy of an excuse for losing my field bag, but I had a beating heart. When it felt safe to move, I tore down that hill as fast as my feet would carry me and never felt so happy as when I stumbled onto my beautiful, safe, rutty road.

B.K. Crawford

Frothing Quicksand

ВЖВ

By the time I reached Bo's place, I was exhausted, thirsty, and feeling stupid.

Everything about the Duke farm screams pig. The whole place is one big mud puddle and when a large drove of pigs move around in their pens, they look like lumps of gooey rock doing a slippery square dance. Grunts, snorts, and squeals mix into a barnyard medley and the smell is enough to put a body in an aroma coma. I made my way behind the third barn where a beautiful pond sits so secluded you'd never know it was there if you didn't know it was there. Some of the biggest catfish in the county come from Duke pond. I supposed no one would mind if I took a quick dip to clean up. I was watching my sneakers float when Bo Duke snuck up behind me, causing me to release a large gas bubble that curled over my hip and broke the surface of the water.

"A little cold for swimming in'it?" He said.

I made a heck of a splash trying to get out of the pond, the ground nothing but slime, and I kept falling back into the water. Bo laughed so hard flecks of mud-cake fell off his

B.K. Crawford

face. Instead of helping me, he just stood there laughing with his hands stuffed in his pockets, watching me wriggle like a frantic worm.

"Holy socks, Bo, gimme a hand."

The surprise on his face would have looked the same if I'd slipped an ice cube down his shirt. He grabbed me by the arm and dragged me out of the pond.

"Heard you had a ruckus the other night," he said, while I brushed pond goo off my jeans.

"Yep, that's why I'm here." I wished for a towel. Who knew goosebumps could grow on goosebumps?

"I thought you came to sell us a Christmas tree," he giggled, and I must have looked confused until he pointed at my head.

I'd forgotten about the twigs I'd planted in my hair for the bear. Lord, I must've looked the sight, but I didn't bother feeling too embarrassed because nobody—and I mean *nobody*—looks as dirty and disheveled as Bo Duke. Bo wears mud like a second skin. There's a year between us, him being the younger, but you'd never know it because he's a foot taller than most boys his age and if you ever need someone to lift a car off your

B.K. Crawford

puppy, Bo's a good choice; I've seen him win a wrestling match against a three ton hog.

I filled him in on the goings on at the Hornbrook house, then told him what I had in mind to do and asked if he wanted to tag along. While it seemed obvious I could no longer trust Joey to keep a secret, Bo would never breathe a word once he swore an oath. He bowed at the waist, waved his arm with a formal flourish and said, "Happy to accomp'ny a purty lady on her adventures." He also said his Pa would have his hide if he left without slopping the hogs, so we spent the next hour hauling buckets of swill. My clothes were nearly dry when we finished feeding the pigs and I itched to get away from the farm fumes and get on with the investigation.

I told Bo what happened with the bear. Naturally, he didn't believe a word of it, but he packed up a lunch for the two of us and we headed out for the Hornbrook house.

"I never even knew a house was here," Bo said when we finally arrived at the Hornbrook place. He snatched up a roll of yellow tape someone dropped on the ground and rushed over so I could see it. 'CRIME SCENE,' it read in bold black letters. I guess since they didn't

B.K. Crawford

find the cowboy's body, the police didn't even bother to stretch the tape out.

"It's dandy, ain't it?" Bo gushed, and shoved the tape into his pocket. I raised an eyebrow but let him keep it, I'd make him share some later. He had me wait at the front door and made me swear I wouldn't go inside without him while he scouted the outside of the house to make sure no one lurked about. I didn't even think of that and scolded myself for not having enough respect for the seriousness of the situation.

When Bo came back he said, "No hide nor hair," and we went inside.

We stood in the kitchen for a few minutes so Bo could take it all in with the same amazement I felt last year when I found the place.

"Where is it?" He finally asked, and I showed him to the trap door in the living room.

"Stinks down here," he snorted.

I looked at him with wonder. How can a boy wearing layers of pig swill smell anything above his own odor? As for the stink in the basement, I had to disagree. Compared to the fumes the rotting corpse put out, the scents I sucked in with Bo seemed refreshing by comparison.

"Come on," I said, "let's get busy. There has to be a clue here somewhere."

Bo took two monster flashlights out of his pack and we began our search.

I felt struck with dumbfounded amazement as I inspected the empty space where the cowboy had hung the last time I stood there; it seemed so odd to find him gone. Daddy was right, though, there were scratch marks on the wall made by the chains and holes where someone had driven pins into the cement. I had a sudden curiosity and took my time carefully inspecting the rest of the walls. I wondered if Daddy had noticed more than one set of pin holes and several areas on the bricks where the scratch marks seemed similar. I certainly couldn't ask him without admitting I'd returned without his permission. To make sure I hadn't imagined or invented things, I double and triple checked the marks. It looked all the world to me like the killer had hung more than one victim in the basement. The small hairs on the back of my neck rose.

This escapade could easily turn into a frothing puddle of quick sand. The truth of

B.K. Crawford

the statement I'd made to Joey on flat rock
when I said we could be next raised the hair
on my arms and I began to tremble like a
mouse staring at cat tonsils. I turned, ready
to tell Bo to pack it all up and let's get the
heck out.

"Com'ere, J.J., look at this."

He stood over a large box of clothing,
holding a small cowboy shirt decked out with
rhinestones against his chest. My eyes went
wide and I made him take every item of
clothing out of the box so we could inspect
them. Everything in the box belonged to a
cowboy costume. The scary thing? Not one
of the items had the smell of must or mold
and most of them still had sales tags hanging
on the cuffs. Care to venture a guess what
store they'd come from? That's right.
Montgomery Ward.

I lifted a few of the sales tags from the
clothes at the bottom of the box and told Bo
to fold the clothes and put them back the
way he found them. I shoved the tags in my
pocket and we scoured the basement, inch
by inch, but found nothing else to help pin
down a killer. Upstairs, we did manage to
find a twenty dollar bill on a bedroom

B.K. Crawford

bureau. Bo stuffed it in his pocket right next to the police tape.

"Hold on, half of that is mine."

"I know," he said, acting all innocent, like he meant to give me half all along.

"Tell ya what, though," I countered, thinking on the fly, "I'll let you have my half if you sell me a field bag and a few digging tools from your garden shed."

He lifted his eyebrows in surprise. "Deal."

"All right, I'll take the field bag today and you can bring the tools to my place tomorrow. Just don't let Daddy see you with them."

We left Hornbook house when we heard that territorial wombat rat squeaking in the walls.

I had one more favor to ask of Bo. I didn't think it wise to go back on Briarhill trail so I asked Bo to go ahead of me and engage Daddy in a conversation so he'd be too busy to see from which direction I'd returned. Risky? Yes, but somehow it felt better than the prospect of being eaten by a bear. When I got back to the house, I found Bo in the kitchen wolfing down the last chocolate chip cookie. Seems Daddy took Joey into town to pick up some spare parts for a lawn mower.

B.K. Crawford

Here's what I wanted to know: How 'purty' could I really be if Bo didn't even save me half a cookie?

B.K. Crawford

Snatching The Catalog
ВЖВ

I reckon Bo got home in time to dole out the afternoon slop and I spent the hour before dinner sitting creek-side, sorting out my thoughts. Two things: First, I planned to sneak Momma's shopping catalog into my bedroom that night so I could check on the prices of those cowboy costumes—see if they were current items. Second, a good archeologist would find out who owned that mess of a house and I thought I knew just which neighborhood busybody might tell me, if I could stand the time it would take to get the information out of her.

The shopping catalog took a complete tour of the house that night as Momma moved it from one room to another before bedtime. Where do you suppose it ended up? That's right, of course it did.

When Daddy's snoring began to saw through the door, I sneaked into my parents' bedroom commando style, elbows crawling across the floor. Arriving bedside, I reached up in the dark and knocked a glass of water off the nightstand. I grunted when the glass bonked me on the head and watched in

B.K. Crawford

horror as a puddle spread out over the floor. To my relief, the glass didn't shatter. I held my breath. Daddy's snoring hiccupped and Momma rolled over, both of them oblivious. I used myself as a human mop—nightgown soaked—finagled the water glass back into its previous position, and snatched the catalog off the nightstand.

Safely back in my room, I checked to make sure Joey was asleep, then changed my pajamas and compared the sales tags to the items in the catalog. Some of the cowboy outfits were still for sale at the same price, which could only mean they were recent purchases, but a few of the tags belonged to discontinued items. So, the costumes in the Hornbrook basement were a mix of old and new. Knowing some of the items were newly purchased put a wrench to my gut.

The feeling of being in over my head returned and I thought about handing over what I'd learned to the police. But, without a body it seemed pointless. In the end, I decided the law wouldn't take me seriously unless I could prove someone died. I thought again about talking to Daddy, but I'd have to come clean about my trickery and deceit. Nope, not gonna happen. Me and Bo were

B.K. Crawford

on our own with this murder investigation, at least for now. But, the horrors of the night weren't over yet, I still had to put the catalog back.

B.K. Crawford

Time With Miss Tilly

ВЖВ

    A light misting rain fell the following day. Now and again, a ray of sunshine would bloom into a rainbow, but mostly the sky churned with a mess of clouds and the air ran cooler than most days in June. I'd get a little wet on the bike ride, but I knew what I had to do. Joey sat in front of the TV, lost in a deep trance. Daddy sat on the porch with a beer in his hand, watching the rain glaze the grass. He didn't give me the least bit of resistance when I told him I wanted to go see Miss Tilly, but looked at me like I'd gone batty. "It's your funeral," he chuckled and waved me off.

    I didn't pack a lunch, Miss Tilly would feed me good once I got to her place. I took my time riding the road, second-guessing myself, not really wanting to go, not minding the rain. With trees on both sides of Moon Street in most spots, very little rain came through anyway. My clothes were only mildly wet when I pulled my bike up to the house and left it leaning against the stairwell that led to her porch.

B.K. Crawford

J. J. HOUSTON ℮58
Murder on Moon Street

I heard her old sing-song voice before I saw her face. "Is that Miss J.J.?" She hollered with excitement.

"Yes, it is, Miss Tilly." I played along like I always do, like I was excited to see her and, oh boy, weren't we gonna have some fun.

Most kids in these parts know you have to be completely crackers to actually volunteer to spend time with Miss Tilly. They say she's one feather short of a loon.

She entered the kitchen wearing a frayed and yellowed bridal gown. High heels, gloves, lacy veil, and most likely a cast iron girdle to hold her inside that thing. She smiled so wide her eyes twinkled and her deep wrinkles doubled. Then, she turned around, quick as she'd come, and left the room, twittering on about how she had something to fit me just right. That was my cue to beat feet out of there. I had plenty of time to do it. I didn't need X-ray vision to know what happened on the other side of the wall. She would bend over that blasted trunk of hers, sift through clothes, and dig until she found the frilliest, most God-awful thing to pull out of the trunk, and I wouldn't hear the end of it until I put it on and played along.

B.K. Crawford

Murder on Moon Street

Instinctively, I moved toward the door. My bike stood less than twenty feet away. I could easily escape before Miss Tilly decided which garment in her trunk held my deepest embarrassment. But I had to find out who owned the Hornbrook house and I didn't know who else to ask without raising suspicions.

She came back holding a bee-keeper's suit—four times my size. I knew my choices. I could protest, insist I wouldn't wear the suit, and go round-and-round with her for an hour, or I could put the suit on and get cracking on the conversation I needed to have with her.

We sat at the kitchen table where she'd put out tea and biscuits. The oversized bee-keeper's helmet kept sliding sideways so that I couldn't see half of what was going on around me, plus I had to lift the net to eat and drink, but I don't suppose that seemed strange to Miss Tilly because she did the same with her moth-eaten wedding veil.

"Grandma," I said, but caught myself before her scowl grew into a deep ravine, "Miss Tilly," I sputtered, correcting my mistake, "Do you know who owns the Hornbrook house up by our place?"

B.K. Crawford

J. J. HOUSTON ©60
Murder on Moon Street

"Sure I do," she said, matter of fact, "But that don't concern us none, put some honey in your tea and let's toast the queen of England. It can't be easy, you know, running the world from a chair without a fluffy cushion, especially if you don't get enough fiber."

Holy socks, I'd come to the right place. Miss Tilly knows who owns the house. Step one complete. Step two would prove the hardest part—dragging the information out of her.

Miss Tilly has no television. There's a radio equipped in her stereo unit, but I've never once heard her play it. She generally skips-to-my-Lou with her Tommy Dorsey, Glenn Miller and Kate Smith albums. So, I figure it's safe to assume she doesn't know about the dead boy we found at the Hornbrook place, because she couldn't possibly, unless someone had come by for a visit. But, like I said, people around here know better than to do that. Once, there was an old man, about a year after Pappy died, who started to come by regularly, but when Daddy found out about him he made it his mission to hunt him down and vowed to cap him in the knees if he ever came around

B.K. Crawford

again. That took care of that and put a bad taste in the mouth of anyone else who might have designs to take advantage of Miss Tilly.

On the other hand, even though she doesn't get visitors, Miss Tilly does seem to know things she shouldn't know. She once told me not to get too angry with my parents because they only want the best for me. Just so happened she said that a day after Momma and me went toe-to-toe in an argument. Momma said I spend too much time with my nose stuck in a book and don't care enough to learn about housekeeping. Which is true. But, how did Miss Tilly know about the argument? Momma didn't call her on the phone and I didn't say a word. Daddy wouldn't come to Miss Tilly's house unless she had a beer keg on the lawn. So, on top of missing half the cards in her deck, Miss Tilly did manage some mystery.

"You hear those sirens the other day?" I asked, biting into my biscuit.

She nodded, but seemed more concerned with whether or not she'd raised her pinky finger high enough over her tea cup to salute the queen of England properly.

I guess she heard the sirens, but paid them no mind. Good. If she knew the seriousness

B.K. Crawford

of the situation, she might not give me information.

She set her teacup down with all the elegance afforded to a woman her age, which is to say her hand trembled slightly, and she said, "Please excuse me for a moment." She then disappeared behind the wall separating the kitchen from the living room where I heard her rifling through her record collection.

Please don't let it be Kate Smith, I thought, pleading for God's divine mercy. I counted my prayer answered when I heard the first notes of *Goodnight Sweetheart*. I suppose Miss Tilly felt this selection might soothe her majesty the queen.

She swayed back into the kitchen where she sashayed, waltzing gracefully, every move calculated, every bend of the knee precarious, but necessary, when dancing among the elite. At least she didn't require me to join her; a sweet reprieve.

Once the song finished and Miss Tilly settled back into her chair to resume the delicate art of tea sipping, I decided to shake her bee's nest a little bit.

B.K. Crawford

"I heard Mr. Flint owns the Hornbrook house and most of the other properties around here, that's why he's so damn rich."

That raised her eyebrows. At least I had her attention.

"We do not use improper language when we are seated with the Queen," she hissed.

I felt my cheeks flush, I had no idea we'd been granted an audience. I wondered if Miss Tilly could see my surprise through the bee netting, but I held my ground. "It must be true."

She sighed and her gaze reached for the ceiling, ever so slightly, her head swaying to the negative. We both knew Mr. Flint didn't own that house.

Miss Tilly soothed my curiosity with one mocking sentence, "Lord, child. They don't call it the Hornbrook house for nothing."

Of course. How could I have been so stupid?

With that, I suspected our audience with her majesty had ended as Miss Tilly ushered the teacups into the sink and asked me to return the bee-keeper's uniform.

Once Miss Tilly put the costumes back in the trunk and silenced the record player, she returned, without the queen.

B.K. Crawford

"Go ask Mr. Charles where he put the stapler. Oh, and take him a new roll," she instructed, handing me a roll of toilet paper and pointing, like I'd forgotten where he's been sitting for as long as I've known him. Once again, I found myself at a pivotal moment. I could argue, as I have so many times in the past and get stuck on the merry-go-round of her dementia, or I could do as she asked, no matter how much my stomach flips when I visit Pappy. I took the toilet paper and made my way across the yard.

On the bright side, the outhouse looked like it might fall apart any day now; the wooden slats grayed, split, warped and spitting out the rusty nails that barely held it together. On the other hand, even if the outhouse did fall apart, Pappy would still be sitting there with his embroidered eyes, pillow-padded chest, and crayon grin. I think Miss Tilly nailed his butt to the seat, or glued it maybe, who knows. I sometimes try to imagine what it felt like to construct his effigy, the sewing, the painting, the crayons; she even thought to use wooden rods to hold his spine and neck straight.

As I understand it, twenty years ago, Pappy went to a doctor who gave him a clean

B.K. Crawford

bill of health, so he up and died that very day of a massive heart attack. A week after his funeral, Miss Tilly lost her last thread of sense and began sewing his replacement. Momma calls the doll, *Raggedy Dad*. She shakes her head, her eyes well up, and then she walks away before anyone can see her cry. I once asked Momma why Miss Tilly keeps Pappy in the outhouse. She answered simply: Because they never got along. Then I wanted to know why she keeps him around at all. Another simple answer: Because she loved him. What a world we live in. Whatever else *Raggedy Dad* is good for, he seems to make good company for Miss Tilly.

I tugged on the outhouse door. The wood is so warped, one tug never makes the grade. Finally, it popped open and I saw him sitting there, bent forward like he had stomach cramps, dark shadows thrown over his face by the long brimmed baseball cap Miss Tilly parked on his head and a chicken—very much alive—pecked at his stuffing. The chicken is Mr. Warble, so named because one of my harebrained cousins trained him to say two words and he never shuts up.

"Shit happens," the chicken declared as I put the toilet paper next to Pappy. I laughed

B.K. Crawford

for two reasons. First, it ain't every day you run into a talking chicken and second, Mr. Warble lost his footing and fell down the unoccupied hole. It's not the first time he'd taken that journey and no way would I reach in to get him out. He'd manage.

I closed the outhouse door and went back to Miss Tilly. Reluctantly, I told her Pappy had no idea where she put the stapler.

"Oh for heaven's sake," she said, exasperated, "He had it last."

I gave her a peck on the cheek and told her I'd come back again soon. She and Pappy would argue over who lost the stapler until she found it, or forgot why she wanted it in the first place.

A single thought occupied my mind during the ride home, how much time and discomfort I could have saved myself if I only had a brain.

B.K. Crawford

The Witch Of Bear Claw Mountain
ВЖВ

The moon seemed shy and in a weepy
mood that night, clouds and fog clinging to its
dim light but not seeming to care too much if
they held on or fell from grace. At least the
rain stopped. I perched on the thin
windowsill in my bedroom and watched the
mist roll, still upset with myself for wasting
time with Miss Tilly when I should have
realized all along the house belonged to a
Hornbrook.

The Hornbrook family seemed thin in my
mind because I have so many cousins it
would take a week to name them all, ours
being a large family stemming from a very
large family. Most of my aunts and uncles
have at least six kids apiece, a few with more.
To the contrary, you can count the
Hornbrooks on one hand and only one lives
nearby—Phoebe Hornbrook, frighteningly
whispered as the witch of Bear Claw
mountain.

Although you might imagine the witch of
Bear Claw mountain an evil, scary looking
woman who lives in a hollowed out tree, that
probably ain't true. A witch? I suspect that's

B.K. Crawford

J. J. HOUSTON ©68
Murder on Moon Street

just bus stop talk, kids with nothing better to
do but try to make each other crap their
drawers. As for what type of woman Phoebe
Hornbrook might be, hell if I know. I've never
been far enough up the hill to get a look at
her, but that's exactly what I had in mind to
do. I thought maybe I'd take Bo along, but
that always meant helping with his chores
and it ain't cordial to go visiting soaked in pig
slop. I decided I'd go on my own and hope
Phoebe Hornbrook could tell me something
useful.

B.K. Crawford

Tendrils Of A Silver Moss

ВЖВ

The following day, I gathered my things and headed for Bear Claw Mountain. Halfway up the hill, I got off my bike when the incline increased too much. I dragged the bike for about three quarters of a mile and then, in frustrated surrender, chose a safe spot alongside the road to leave it behind. Huffing and puffing, I decided to take a breather. Looking behind me, I felt a rush of excitement at the thought of riding back down the hill. Ain't nothing like going downhill with the wind whipping against your cheeks, the world speeding by in a blur. What a hoot.

The sun couldn't decide if it wanted to come out or hide under the covers playing peek-a-boo. I wished it would make up its mind.   When the light hit the ground, it dazzled the tufts of white mountain laurel splattering the hillside and illuminated patches of wild strawberries. The berries had no chance of survival because they're my favorite treat. The higher I went, the sweeter the berries, and I wished I'd had a pint box or two so I could take some to Miss Tilly, who,

B.K. Crawford

despite her crumbled crackers, makes an award-winning strawberry pie. Maybe Phoebe Hornbrook had containers to lend. My mouth watered at the prospect.

All-in-all, it took two hours to scale the mountain. In fairness, though, I would have gotten there quicker if I hadn't stopped to rob so many berry patches along the way.

I knew my trek had nearly come to an end when I saw smoke rising over the birches and pines. Smoke will always make you stop and wonder. June normally isn't a month for burning wood in a fireplace, but folks around here do plenty of burning otherwise. Some burn grass to get it to grow richer the next season, and some burn papers and other garbage in burning barrels. It's not uncommon to see the deep, dark, smoke of burning tires either. The wisps I saw weren't thick enough for a house fire, thank God.

I trudged along, moving closer to the source of the fire. The road grew thinner and began to wind to the right where it turned into a footpath. Needless to say, this is where anyone driving a vehicle gives up and walks the rest of the way. Here, the trees grew closer together, darkening the path, and setting a chill to my bones. Vigorous

B.K. Crawford

vines grouped together to form a twisted
canopy over my head, so dense the sun had
no hope to break through—I wondered if this
happened naturally, or if someone had
trained the vines. It looked eerie, and I felt as
though I'd entered a living tunnel. The
thought crossed my mind to turn back and go
home, but I pinched myself and trudged on. I
hadn't come this far to chicken out.

I could smell the smoke now. Not wood.
Wood has a distinctive earthen odor. Not
tires, but I knew that, the smoke didn't rise
dark enough. Not trash, trash has an acidic
stink. Wasn't barbeque, because barbeque
makes me drool. Still, it did smell like
cooking of some sort, but my nose couldn't
pin a tag on it. I supposed I'd find out soon
enough.

I saw her hair before anything else. It
seemed to me like the tendrils of a silver
moss, long and gliding on the wind, lifting off
her shoulders by vigorous gusts and resting
there again when the wind lost its temper.
She wore a long skirt that curled around her
ankles and a cheerful cape to keep the wind
at bay. She stood stirring a bubbling liquid in
a vat hung over a robust fire. Nothing about

B.K. Crawford

her seemed odd or off, and my confidence renewed.

"Hello," I called, louder than I might if the wind weren't whipping, and raised my hand to wave at her.

Startled, her head turned sharply toward the sound. She squinted as if her eyesight failed her and she jutted her head forward. I moved out of the twisted tunnel and into full view, where she could see me better. When she smiled, I exhaled with relief and felt my shoulders drop.

"Hello," she muttered, demurely.

I continued to cross the lawn toward her, slowly drawing closer.

"Are you Phoebe Hornbrook?"

She nodded, her gray eyes opening wide to look me over. I fixed her age at about sixty-five or so, almost as old as Miss Tilly.

I conjured as much of a casual tone as I could muster, "I came to ask you about the old Hornbrook house on Moon Street."

I saw her face harden against my inquiry and noticed a pile of bones resting at her feet.

The urge to run hit me like a bolt of lightning, but I held my ground. The bones

B.K. Crawford

could belong to an animal. She *was* cooking, after all.

I stood close enough now to see inside the vat. A milky white substance, bubbling with a thick boil.

"What ya cooking?" I did my best to hold my composure and seem as neighborly as possible, still hoping to borrow a basket or two for strawberries.

She smiled again, a grandmotherly grin that lifted her wrinkled cheeks to her eyes and made them sparkle.

"Nosey children," she answered, sweet as can be.

I imagine I must have looked like a total blur as I bolted back into the twisted tunnel. The sound of her laughter haunted me until I'd run far enough for the wind to carry the mocking tones away.

B.K. Crawford

What Everyone Else Knows
ВЖВ

   The next afternoon, Bo and I took our lunch outside under the poplar tree where we could talk and sip cold apple cider while we named the shapes of the clouds. I saw a rabbit, but Bo argued, insisting it was a dragon. "Get your own cloud," I scolded.

   I've heard Bo yuck it up plenty of times over the years, he's tickled by the slightest thing, but I never heard him laugh so hard as when I claimed the stories about the witch of Bear Claw mountain were all true and how I came to know it. Tears ran down his face, leaving streaks in the mud and you could actually see white skin peeking out from underneath. He didn't seem to have enough wind between guffaws to keep him from gasping and, at one point, I thought he might hark in his stew, which would be an awful shame because Mrs. Duke makes a delicious beef stew.

   I waited with all the patience of a soldier clutching a live hand grenade for Bo's laughing fit to pass.

   "You should've asked me to come along," he said, once he could talk again.

B.K. Crawford

I made a face, hoping to express my annoyance at his incessant belief that I needed a hero.

"No," he shook his head, "I could have told you what she was cooking. You wasted a trip up the mountain because you don't know about her like I do."

"Oh, you know her, do you? You know things about the witch of Bear Claw mountain, stuff no one else knows?" I sounded a little snotty.

"No. But I do know what everyone else knows. Everyone but you." He laughed.

I shoved a big bite of stew into my mouth and let the beef melt on my tongue. Lord, I wish my mother had this recipe.

"What does everyone except me know?" I asked, mouth still full.

He waited a long while before he answered. Not because he was busy eating, but to torture me with the wait. I rolled my eyes and shook my head, like I didn't care what he had to say. That always does the trick.

"She comes off the mountain once a month to deliver loads of soap to the grocery store. Has her own brand. I bet you even have a bar in your bathroom, most folks

B.K. Crawford

around here do. That's how she makes her living. She was cooking soap when you went up there yesterday."

"Didn't smell like soap," I said, washing my stew down with a swig of cider.

"Soap doesn't smell like soap until you put the essence in it, she probably hadn't done that yet."

"What about the bones, smartass? Those weren't there by accident."

Bo took his napkin off his lap and used it to wipe a little stew drizzle from my mouth. I was saving that for later.

"It's tradition in old circles to use bone marrow in soap making. Maybe you don't spend enough time in the library, brainy girl."

I took a swipe at him, but he expected it and moved out of the way in time to avoid getting whopped on the head.

"She told me she was cooking kids," I griped.

"I would've run, too," he said, but only to make me feel better about being a chickenshit.

B.K. Crawford

Invading The Dig

ВЖВ

After my picnic with Bo, I went home to find Daddy and Joey bent over the kitchen table, murmuring. The whispering, I supposed, meant Momma had gone to take a nap.

I made a beeline for the kitchen and gasped with surprise when I saw what they were fussing about. For the longest time, I stood there staring at the items they were examining on the table. Three Indian arrowheads, a little copper pot with strange etchings, and a lizard with a coiled tail, small enough to fit on a necklace, carved out of a clear piece of crystal. My field bag and excavation tools lay perched at Joey's feet. Someone, it seemed, had raided my dig on Briarhill. My blood began to boil and I felt an overwhelming urge to rip Joey's head off his shoulders, especially when a cocky, neener-neener grin bloomed on his face.

"You found those at the Briarhill caves?" I said, calm as a purring kitten.

He nodded and chuckled.

B.K. Crawford

"Good for you, Joey." I offered him a high-five, which he declined, a certain confusion washing over his face.

"Knock yourself out." I walked away, acting as if I couldn't care less and went to my room.

That rotten little son-of-a-prick, I thought as I plopped down on the lower bunk. The nerve of him, invading my dig and taking artifacts out of there without my permission. Ready to blow, the volcano in my head broiled and I suddenly understood why Daddy kept his firearms under lock and key.

I wanted to go to Daddy and complain, remind him he'd given the dig to me and me alone, then make him promise to keep Joey away from the caves, but I knew exactly what he'd say. He'd say I'd been neglecting the dig, he'd say I should have tended to it. Too true. Damn it all to hell and back.

A creak on the stairs alerted me, so I grabbed a book from the floor and opened it up in the middle. By the time Joey reached the doorway, I had my nose buried in the book.

"Awesome stuff, huh?" He gloated.

"Yeah, it's awesome." I flipped a page.

"I bet it's worth a fortune," he pushed.

B.K. Crawford

"Nope." I turned another page. "I've got plenty just like it and it ain't worth a dime."

He expelled a sigh.

"It's fun digging it up, though," I said, as if to encourage him to go on digging.

"How come you stopped going up there?"

"Got bored. Better things to do."

"Really? You still chasing killers?" He sounded smug.

"Nope, too dangerous. Mr. Flint's taking a bunch of campers to the mountains for the summer. The Missus said they had room for one more. I told her I'd let her know, but I think I'll go along. It's sure to be a hoot and a half."

He leaned against the door frame. "When are they leaving?"

I flipped another page. "Tomorrow."

"I hope y'all have a good time," he said and left.

The fast-fluttered thumping on the stairwell told me something had him in a rush.

B.K. Crawford

J. J. HOUSTON ©80
Murder on Moon Street

At dinner that night, Joey bragged about how the Flints invited him to go to the mountains with them. I glared and pouted, pouted and glared until he left convinced he'd completely ticked me off.

B.K. Crawford

The Crystal Skulls
ВЖВ

I've read enough books on archeology to know what happens when you find something of value, historically or otherwise, on an archeological dig: The Feds and the museum experts move in to take over your dig. Not only will they confiscate the dig, they'll also take credit for its discovery and any money associated with it. Suddenly, you're not even allowed to snoop around your own dig, especially if you're just a kid from the boondocks. So, if you're into this stuff like I am, and if you know what's good for you, take a note from J.J. Houston's journal and keep quiet about it.

The crystal lizard Joey unearthed was no slouching trinket. I examined it for hours and hours and couldn't find a single seam in the piece, not a crack, not a blemish. Whoever carved it, did it to perfection, without lifting the knife, or whatever tool they'd used to create it. I doubted, very much, the same culture that made the arrowheads crafted the crystal because you could see cut marks all over the arrowheads. The only pieces I've ever read about that were anywhere near

B.K. Crawford

the quality of the lizard are the famed Crystal Skulls. Thirteen skulls, all-in-all. Legend has it, if the skulls are ever united in one place they'll demonstrate a mysterious power. Some say they open a portal from one dimension to another, but opinions on the subject are more plentiful than grains of sand in the desert and it's hard to separate myth from fact. I wondered if the crystal lizard had any cryptic power.

Truth is, if Joey had alerted anyone to what he'd found, for whatever reason, the Feds would have cordoned off my dig lickety split.

I took the lizard to Daddy and told him everything I knew and even confessed to tricking Joey into going with the Flints on their camping trip. He listened to everything I had to say, nodded once or twice and even grinned when I confessed. He promised to find ways to keep Joey off Briarhill if the boy had any inkling to go back up there after he came back from the mountains. My Daddy is a loose cannon sometimes, but like I said before, he ain't stupid.

The coolest part? Daddy said if he could make time, he might come along for some more father-daughter digs.

B.K. Crawford

I felt certain about one thing, I needed to get back to those caves to see what else I could uncover. At the same time, I couldn't give up on finding out what happened to that poor little cowboy in the basement of the Hornbrook house. We still had a killer on the loose.

B.K. Crawford

J. J. HOUSTON ©84
Murder on Moon Street

An Unexpected Visitor
ВЖВ

Daddy and Momma decided to drive to town to pick up parts for a new repair job Daddy wrangled. They asked if I wanted to go along, even said they'd stop at the A&W if I liked. While I do love root beer, sloppy burgers, and watching clumsy waitresses fall off their skates, I'm not much for towns and I usually won't go unless I have to.

Not ten minutes after Momma and Daddy left, a strange car pulled up in front of the house. Shiny and new, I couldn't imagine who it belonged to. Unnerved, I stared. The person in the driver's seat sat in the black Buick for a long time before stepping out. I'd been sitting on the porch, reading a copy of *Great Expectations*, my summer reading assignment. I had to finish a book report before school opened in the fall and I'd have to fit in at least a chapter a day to get it done on time.

A woman in a sharp navy blue pantsuit stepped out of the car. Military? My heart skipped a beat. Even after I got a good look at her, I still had no idea who she was. Early thirties, brown hair in a tight bun, clipboard

B.K. Crawford

in hand, stern look on her face, and I immediately decided she looked like a teacher.

She strode slowly over the lawn on her way to the porch, moving her head side-to-side as she took everything in. Not much to see really, just Daddy's garden, the hammock swinging between two large trees up by the road, a large lilac bush, some planter boxes Momma put out, the tractor Daddy took apart for repair, and Crusher lazing in the sun. She stopped walking when she saw the dog.

"He don't bite," I said.

She walked a wide curve around him anyway, just in case, I suppose.

"My folks aren't home," I told her, figuring she'd turn right back around and hit the road.

"I'm here to see you." She reached into her pocket and pulled out a badge.

Holy socks, a cop.

She slipped the badge back into her pocket, sat down next to me on the step and said, "My name is Lieutenant Shafer, you can call me Kate."

Honestly, I couldn't think of a reason I'd want to call her anything but gone. I don't trust authority figures. Way I see it, they all

B.K. Crawford

popped out of their mommas just as slippery as I did. There's something fishy about a person who thinks they're better than anyone else and I don't care why. Plus, I had a bad taste in my mouth for cops after the way them boys treated us when Joey and me reported the body at the Hornbrook house.

"I'm with the homicide division of the State Police," she informed me. I suspect the law required her to say so.

"Somebody die?"

She inhaled real deep and puckered her lips a little. I think she knew I was messing with her.

"I'm not here to give you a hard time, Jennifer."

She noticed me recoil at the use of my proper name.

"What do your friends call you?"

"Stubborn, stupid, and ugly," I mumbled sarcastically. "J.J., for Jennifer Jane."

"Okay, J.J. I just wondered if you might tell me a little more about what you saw last week at the abandoned house?"

"I can't tell you any more than what's in your reports." I said it mean like, so she'd know to back off.

B.K. Crawford

"Look," she said, probably annoyed with me, "I know what it's like to be a kid with something important to say and have no one willing to listen. I'm here for you. Us girls have to stick together." She playfully poked me in the leg with her pen as she summed up her line of manure.

I thought about telling her where she could find a body and send her off to Miss Tilly's outhouse, but part of me suspected she might take Pappy away. The law is cruel like that and I wouldn't want to upset Miss Tilly just to pull a prank.

I closed my book and stood up. "Do I need to call a lawyer?"

The wheels on the Buick spun out when she pulled away.

Daddy's nostrils flared when he found out how the cop lady tried to get information out of me. I told him I didn't know why I acted so mean toward her and I apologized for that, but he said he was proud as all get-out for the way I handled it. Something about her just felt off to me. Momma tells me to pay attention to feelings like that, it's intuition she says, and insists it's good for a person to trust their instincts.

B.K. Crawford

Fetching The Mail

ВЖВ

Thunder rattled every window in the house and darkness reigned for two and a half days, the only light in the sky came from bolts of lightning that zapped off the arms of a good many trees.

I can't say I like storms. It ain't so much the fear that rips through my bones every time God drops a bowling ball, but more the frustration and cramped feeling of being stuck inside, especially when I had so much to do. I took advantage of the time by finishing my reading assignment and writing the report; one less thing hanging over my head.

A whole week had passed since me and Joey found that boy's body and I hadn't come any nearer to solving the case than when I started. I still saw the dead cowboy hanging on the wall in my dreams. As much as I tried not to, I wondered what it must have been like to die that way, tortured in some lunatic's basement. I wondered who the boy was, how the killer got hold of him, and if his Momma was out there somewhere, crying in

B.K. Crawford

her apron, missing that boy with a heart full of ache.

Round about noon, the storm let up and although the wind still threw a fit, the skies began to clear, allowing the first rays of sunlight to peek through. Our front yard had become nothing but an overgrown puddle, so I slipped on a pair of rubber boots and went outside in search of rainbows.

Hot and muggy, another Saturday in June, summer in the hills.

The mailbox choked on an oversized load. No one had been out to get the mail for two days, what with the rain and all, so I sloshed up to the road and relieved the box of its burden.

Ma Bell—Telephone bill.

Donation request from the local church—Fire kindling.

Complimentary copy of a new newspaper looking for regular subscribers—Ain't happening here.

Postcard from the camp site—Seems it didn't take Joey long to figure out the campers who went with the Flints all belonged to the same Girl Scout troop. He promised me payback. I laughed out loud at the angry scrawl he wrote on the card.

B.K. Crawford

J. J. HOUSTON ©90
Murder on Moon Street

Typed letter addressed to Jennifer Jane Houston—Tucked that under my arm pit.

Late tax notice for Daddy—Automatic bad mood.

A new shopping catalog for Momma—Automatic good mood.

A flier from the Young Reader's Library addressed to me—A list of one hundred awesome books I'd love to read but can't afford.

A Real Estate flier advertising houses for sale, $2,000 shacks to $25,000 mansions—What a waste of a good stamp.

Flier from the local car dealership—Another wasted stamp.

A brown package from Howard's Auto Parts addressed to Mr. Denver Houston—Something heavy rattled inside, a part Daddy needed for his repair business.

A long envelope trimmed in red, white, and blue. Airmail from Denny Junior—Quiet weeping would replace Momma's good mood.

I'm not an only child, just the youngest and the only one left at home. Denny Junior, Danny, and Dale are my older brothers and they're all off fighting in Vietnam. My sisters, Jeannie and Jackie are off chasing their

B.K. Crawford

dreams. Jeannie is learning how to be a nurse and Jackie is training race horses at a farm down near Harrisburg. We get phone calls and letters all the time from my sisters, but it's a rare treat to hear anything from the boys.

Truth be told, when that cop lady showed up the other day, I prayed to God she wasn't military. You hear stories all the time about how the army sends people you don't even know to come say somebody died on the battlefield. Scares the hell out of a military family when a strange car pulls up. That's why I wanted to believe that woman was just a teacher. Never dreamed she was a cop.

While Denny Junior's letter would surely make Momma sad about him being so far away, we'd all be happy to know he still had fire in his kick.

I handed the mail to Daddy and went upstairs to read my letter.

Postmark: Boontown. But that didn't tell me anything. Heck, you can send a letter to your next-door neighbor and it'll still take forever to arrive because it has to go to Boontown first. Government efficiency.

I ripped the envelope open, pulled out the paper inside and unfolded it.

B.K. Crawford

My pulse quickened and my stomach flipped so bad I almost lost my lunch. Someone had used different sized ink stamps to write:

'Keep your nose out of it or you're next.'

I immediately thought I should show the letter to Daddy. I'd even made it halfway down the stairs when I stopped to think it over. If I showed him the letter, he'd know I'd meddled in the case. I'd have to tell him I'd gone back to the house after he told me not to. If I didn't tell him, he couldn't protect me. Trembling, I went back to my room and soaked my pillow with quiet tears.

I needed a plan of action. The letter changed everything. I couldn't deal with this without backup and a witness. If the killer did manage to snatch me, someone had to know why. It seemed far too dangerous to keep the information to myself.

Daddy didn't blink twice when I said I'd decided to go help Bo with his chores.

B.K. Crawford

Chasing Clues

ВЖВ

Bo leaned over the kitchen table, staring at a colorful flier, smiling ear-to-ear. When he saw me walk into the room, he snatched up the flier and waved it in front of my face.

"The county carnival," he gushed. "Starts a week from today. Thanks to you, I've got enough money to go."

Damn, I shouldn't have let him keep that twenty-dollar bill all to himself. He might have money to spend at the carnival, but I didn't.

I reminded myself I had bigger things to think about than whether or not I had the money to win a stuffed bear I had no use for.

Just then, a curious thought crossed my mind.

"You still have that twenty-dollar bill?"

"Sure do," he gloated.

"Can I see it? I won't take it from you or anything. I said it's yours and it is. I just want to look at it."

He pulled his billfold from his back pocket.

"You're sure this is the same exact bill we found at the Hornbrook place?"

"It ain't like they grow on trees."

B.K. Crawford

J. J. HOUSTON ©94
Murder on Moon Street

"I only ask because it's important."

"I promise, it's the same bill."

"Okay, lay it flat on the table."

He did as I requested.

I gave it a good once-over.

"Look at the date."

He picked up the bill and squinted, "Nineteen-sixty-three. Oh, dear Lord." He sputtered. "It's a brand new bill, issued this year."

I offered a solemn nod.

We found the bill on the main floor of the house in one of the bedrooms. It seemed strange for a killer to use that room. Rats had stolen the stuffing from the mattress long ago and even if they hadn't, no roof remained. Anyone lying on the bed would see nothing but sky overhead. Leaving a fresh bill on the dresser made no sense at all.

"I don't supposed you'd let me have the bill for safe keeping? It could be an important clue."

Bo's face darkened into a grave expression. "I need it for the carnival," he whined, but then his face went suddenly bright. "Hold up a second." He rushed out of the room.

B.K. Crawford

When he came back, he had his Daddy's Polaroid camera in hand. We quickly photographed both sides of the bill and returned the camera before anyone might notice it gone. Bo let me keep the photos because I let him keep the money.

I asked if we could go to the barn for a bit and we stepped out into the sun. It would take a day or two of intense heat to dry up the mess the thunderstorm made. Our feet made sucking sounds as we trudged through the mud and Bo laughed when it sounded especially gross. I might've laughed too, but the letter in my pocket weighed on me like a massive boulder.

We sat on two large bales of hay. The sun poured through cracks in the barn slats and lit up the scattered hay at our feet so that it beamed like strands of gold.

"I can't let you keep this a secret," Bo gasped, after he read the letter.

"I'm not keeping it secret. I showed it to you, didn't I?"

"You know what I mean, J.J. This is too big for us. You're in deep, deep trouble."

"I know, but I can't tell Daddy, he'll have my hide."

B.K. Crawford

Bo's face went soft. I knew he understood what I meant. Everyone in these parts knows my Daddy has a mean streak. But, just as fast as Bo had gone soft, his expression cemented again.

"Here's the difference. Now you pay close attention and listen up."

He sounded like one of those starched and pressed cops.

"Your Daddy will probably be upset, he might even whip your hide, might even lock you up for the rest of the summer. But, he doesn't want to see you *dead*. Whoever wrote this letter does. That's a mighty big difference."

I saw his point, I really did. But I needed him to see my side of things. "If I get locked up for the summer, no one else will search for the murderer. There's no body, Bo. No body, no case. That's how the cops see it. Locked up or not, I'm already next on the list." I waved the envelope to emphasize my point. "I have to nab the killer before he gets to me. There has to be a way to do that without telling Daddy," I complained. "There just has to."

B.K. Crawford

Bo gave it a good deal of thought and remained silent as a devout mouse for the longest time.

"Come on with me," he finally said, standing up and reaching for my hand. He pulled me to my feet and took me back to the kitchen where he rooted around until he found what he wanted.

"This is today's paper," he said, flipping through the pages.

"There. Right there," he said, excited. "Look at that."

I had to shoo his tapping finger away so I could read the lines beneath it.

An obituary for a local boy. Davey Newhouse, age eight, died unexpectedly, no photograph.

I raised my eyebrows in confusion. "So?"

He stuffed his thumbs into his belt loops. "So, when you move a decomposed body, you have to do something with it. I don't imagine you'd want to take it home to have dinner with it, so you'd probably dump it somewhere quick...on account of the unappealing aroma. Then, someone might find it. Then, there'd be a funeral," he pointed at the newspaper.

B.K. Crawford

My eyes went wide and I took in a sharp breath. "You think this kid might be the cowboy from the basement?"

"Can't say for sure," Bo said, scratching his head. "But I've been watching the obituaries for a week straight and this is the first one that might match. And, look at that," he pointed to the section of the obituary that said the memorial services would be held tomorrow afternoon at a church located just a spit and a whistle from my place.

"If you could get to the service and get a peek at that kid, you might know if it was the same boy or not."

He had a good point. I did want to know who that poor boy was. It wouldn't be difficult to identify the corpse, the skeleton I saw had a shattered cheek. That would tell all. I couldn't say if knowing the victim's identity could really help me find the killer, but it sure wouldn't hurt.

I thought about it while I helped Bo slop the hogs. When we finished his chores, I asked if he wanted to come to the memorial service with me. He nervously rubbed his face and a slab of mud fell off his cheek, looking everything like a piece of plaster crumbling off a wall. While I might manage

B.K. Crawford

to skulk around the service unnoticed, Bo would stick out like a dirty thumb.

"Never mind," I said, "I'll manage."

"No." He took a deep breath. "I'll go with you. But let's get there an hour early, before anyone else shows up. The body should be there by then and we won't have to dress up or deal with..."

"Soap?"

"No," he blushed, "with curious adults."

Impressive. Really good thinking. I nodded and agreed to his terms.

Before I left the Duke farm, Bo took me by the shoulders and looked me straight in the eye.

"I ain't the kind of man to tell a woman what to do," he looked serious as mustard on rye, "but, I gotta say, you need to think about that letter good and hard. I won't stand by and let someone kill my girl, even if it means ratting behind your back."

"Your girl?"

"Don't blame me for destiny." A slight grin played at the corners of his mouth.

"I'm older than you," I declared.

"I'm taller than you," he countered.

"I'll think about the letter. Don't you dare tell anybody anything. Hear me, Bo?"

B.K. Crawford

He shook his head. "Can't make no promises. I'll try to keep it under wraps for now. If you get any more letters, though, don't hold out on me."

I promised I'd tell him if I got another letter and told him he had some thinking to do, too, because any 'man' worth his salt would surely ask 'his girl' to attend the county carnival with him.

Riding through the mud on the way home, I decided one thing. I had to find the identity of this killer before someone decked me out in an Annie Oakley costume and pinned me to a cement wall.

B.K. Crawford

A Sad Box
ВЖВ

There's a knoll on the left side of the road next to the church. Twenty yards from the church door, the hill is fronted by tall tufts of untended grass. Bo and I peeked through the grass, waiting for the two men who had marched a coffin into the church to come back out; which, we hoped, would leave the church deserted for a while before mourners came to pay their respects.

The sun seemed in a blistering mood and Bo's bologna began to sweat. It looked to me like he'd packed a whole pound, but he didn't offer a single sliver to me. He tore off strips of meat, shoved them into his face, and mindlessly hummed the bologna jingle while we stared at the church door. Now and again, a car would turn onto Moon Street and, while the drivers slowed down to ogle the hearse, we'd duck down, two unseen phantoms, nervous about what we might find once we got inside the church.

The men came out, parked the hearse in a field across the street, then jumped into a pickup and took off.

B.K. Crawford

I looked at Bo. He swallowed hard. *Now or never.*

Bo took a small crowbar out of his pack and shoved the bag into the grass where no one would see it.

"What's that for?" I asked, afraid of the answer.

"In case it's a closed coffin." He said it like it should have been obvious. It wasn't.

We didn't have time to argue. I stood and pushed past the hill with Bo following close behind. We made a rush for the door and went inside.

I don't know why I expected a dark church, but the sun filtered through the stained glass windows and lit the place up beautifully.

We rushed past the pews to the coffin parked in front of the pulpit. A small box, a plain box—a sad box—perched atop a metal platform.

A closed coffin, as Bo had predicted, and no amount of tugging on our part could open it. Bo raised his eyebrows in an I-told-you-so expression and pulled the crowbar from his back pocket.

"Be careful, don't mark it up. We don't want anyone to know it's been opened."

B.K. Crawford

Bo nodded and I nervously blabbered while he worked the hinges.

"Just a quick peek and we're out of here," I prattled.

I heard a crack and a pop.

"Oh, God, don't split the wood," I begged, my head jerking this way and that, mostly behind us, for fear someone might come through the door.

"Doing my best," Bo mumbled.

I heard another pop.

"That should do it." He put the crowbar down so he could lift the coffin lid. I held my breath. What if it wasn't the right kid? What if we broke in for nothing?

I needn't have worried. Shattered cheek and all, I gaped at the same skeleton I'd seen hanging in the Hornbrook basement.

Bo shrieked when he saw the corpse and pushed away from the coffin with so much force, the casket toppled over with a deafening crash, spilling the kid onto the floor where his skull rolled away from the rest of the remains, settling somewhere under the first row of pews. Bo tripped over his own feet and screamed like a little girl.

We had to run. Bo had immense strength, but not enough to lift the casket all by

B.K. Crawford

himself. His state of mind left something to be desired as well. We'd never get things back in place before someone showed up for the services. Grabbing Bo by the arm, I practically dragged him out the door.

"I'm so sorry," I blurted as we stumbled over the corpse; a vibrant young boy reduced to a sack of bones stuffed into his favorite pair of pajamas, minus a skull.

Gasping, we fell into our hiding place at the base of the knoll. Bo looked like he might upchuck. A perfectly normal reaction for someone who had seen what he'd just seen.

Come to find out, that's not what had him rattled. I felt my oily luck run out when he sputtered, "I left the crowbar inside."

Without a thought, I burst to my feet and went back inside to rescue the crowbar. On the way out of the church, I saw a black Buick pull into the parking lot.

I got to Bo as fast as I could and we took the back way, running along the creek bed, to get to my place. It wouldn't do for someone to see us hoofing down the road, running from the church.

Bo squealed, "Aww *hell*," the entire way. I spent the time trying to remember where I'd seen that black Buick. My stomach did a

B.K. Crawford

cartwheel when it came to me. *The cop lady.*
Why had she gone to Davey Newhouse's
service? Did she see me darting away from
the church with a crowbar in my hand? Holy
socks, I hoped not.

B.K. Crawford

Do You Know This Boy?

ВЖВ

Bo sat next to me beside the creek until he'd calmed down enough to get on home. I stayed to watch the mermaid moss flowing on the rocks in the creek bed. So many questions stampeded through my mind, I could barely keep track of them. On top of that, I couldn't stop thinking about how horrified the people attending Davey Newhouse's services would be when they saw him spilled on the floor like that. I felt like I'd been nabbed at the grocery store with a can of oysters stuffed in my purse.

I knew I had to get past the nagging guilt, so I told myself, what's done is done and, no matter how much I wanted to, I couldn't undo it—not a miracle cure, but it helped me focus.

It seemed strange Davey Newhouse could go missing in these parts without a peep from the neighbors. Were the adults in the community whispering to keep the young from hearing, or did they not know about Davey? There's always a call for help when someone goes missing and it's never long before a neighborhood search is underway.

B.K. Crawford

Murder on Moon Street

Folks around here will turn every rock until they find what they're looking for.

I threw a pebble into the creek and listened to it plop. Miss Tilly would have said something. I don't know how she does it, she doesn't get out much and she doesn't read the papers or listen to the radio, but somehow that woman knows exactly what's going on around her all the time. She would have cautioned me to be careful if she'd known anything about a missing kid. Come to think of it, most parents would lock their kids inside if they knew they had a killer on the loose. How could they not know?

Something about all of this just didn't add up.

I heard Daddy call my name and jumped to my feet. I could tell from his tone his bees were swarming.

Ain't no use trying to guess what might have Daddy pounding the war path. It could be anything from toothpaste spatter on the bathroom mirror to money missing from his wallet. For the record, I never touch his wallet, but it wouldn't hurt me to be more careful with the toothpaste.

As I stepped around the side of the house, I saw the trouble right away. The cop lady

B.K. Crawford

had parked her black Buick beside our mailbox and stood next to Daddy, waiting on me. For what seemed like a very long time, I stared at her, unable to move, convinced she'd throw me in jail for vandalizing the church.

"Lieutenant Shafer has some questions she wants to ask." Daddy looked mad as a wet cat and motioned for me to come on.

My knees refused to cooperate. After a long pause, she stepped forward. Daddy followed, stride for stride.

"Do you know this boy?" She handed me the photograph of a young, gap-toothed boy with red hair. He wore a formal suit and tie, and his smile beamed like he had more than two presents under the tree.

I looked close and took my time. "I might've seen him on the school bus once or twice. I think he lives up on the hill with the rich folks. He doesn't ride the bus much because his Daddy drives him to school."

The cop lady nodded. "Did you ever talk to him? Did he ever tell you anything scary?"

"No," I blurted. "Him and his sister are both in a younger grade. I don't even know their names. Hardly saw them at school and, like I said, they didn't ride the bus much. Did he run away? Is he missing? Did he do something bad?"

Instead of answering, she asked another question, "Have you been by the church today?"

I didn't have time to think about how I might answer, because Daddy took me by the arm and pulled me to his side.

"It ain't Sunday," he said, aggravated.

She waited for me to answer on my own, but I didn't say a word. So, she left her calling card with Daddy, told him to call if anyone else asked about the boy in the photograph, and took off.

"You know that kid?" Daddy barked as he dragged me into the house and slammed the door.

"Nope," I answered, truthful as can be. "Do you know who he is, Daddy?"

Daddy curled his lips and shook his head, no.

Now, here's what I wanted to know. Had the Lieutenant shown me a picture of Davey Newhouse, or a photograph of a kid just gone missing? I suspected a missing boy, because I couldn't see why the police would look for a kid already dead and sprawled over the

B.K. Crawford

church floor. So, I asked Daddy if we'd have a neighborhood search. He said no, because the Lieutenant never said the boy was missing.

That made no sense in my mind because what else is a kid you can't find, if he ain't missing?

I needed a school photograph with that boy in it. They print the names of the students underneath the picture. Too young, the boy wasn't in my class, so my photos offered no help. He wasn't in Bo's class neither, so his photos wouldn't help. I didn't know any of the younger kids in the neighborhood and school wouldn't open again until fall. I'd have to find another way.

At dinner that night, Daddy asked if I'd like to dig at the caves the following day, said he'd been thinking about going up there ever since Joey found the crystal lizard. What could I say?

A Spectacular Find
вжв

The Briarhill caves really aren't far from our house, but because you have to climb a massive hill to get to them, it takes over an hour to cover a mile. The journey starts out in the open field we use for sledding and by the time you reach the top of the hill you need a good, long rest.

Just past the crest of the hill, there's a patch of forest we call the Little Jungle because the vines growing between the trees are thick and seem to grow faster than magic mushrooms. If my brave and adventurous brothers hadn't forged a path, years ago, it would take forever to cut through the knotted vines. Even now, there's no way to get through without stopping to whack down new growth.

Once the trials and tribulations of the Little Jungle are over, you'll find yourself standing on the edge of Copper pond. I was six or seven years old when my brothers, Danny and Dale, first took me there. It's a good sized watering hole surrounded by cattail reeds that stand tall and proud like soldiers guarding ancient treasures.

B.K. Crawford

The water is the murky color of copper and it's always covered in shadow because of the surrounding trees. Naturally, I shied away when I first saw it. It looked scary. Not one to miss an opportunity, Danny told me he once saw a slimy, old monster lurking beneath the muddy waters. Gachoo, he called it, and said the monster had grown almost as big as the pond itself and it only ate meat. Seeing how frightened I'd become, Dale jumped onboard and told me never to put so much as a toe in the water or, "Gachoo will *get you*." Since the pond doesn't look inviting enough for a swim anyway, I've never tested the waters. Not even after I realized the boys were only poking fun.

I stood staring at the surface of the metallic water, not catching so much as a ripple, when Daddy gave me a nudge to get a move on. We had another wide batch of forest to tackle before we arrived at the caves.

Every time I come near the Briarhill caves, it's like I'm seeing them for the first time. Electricity builds under my skin, tickling my arms and lifting the hair on the back of my neck. I think Daddy feels the wonder of this

B.K. Crawford

place, too. He stands perfectly still beside me, taking in the oldness of it, sensing the spirits that long to be remembered, and the solemn sanctity that courses through every rock, every leaf, every root, and even the soil. We each take several deep breaths, paying our respects to the land and its history, to those who came before us, to those who allow us to wander here—keepers of the past.

Daddy is first to break the trance as he begins searching the ground for signs of trespass. It didn't take him long to identify which cave Joey had entered on his last visit. Daddy motioned for me to come see the perfect imprints of Joey's size six shoes positioned just outside the largest cave.

There are seven caves in all, but only three large enough to enter without having to crawl. The largest of the caves is situated in the middle, while the bookend caves (as I call them) are squat and hard to enter, best suited for a temporary wildlife refuge and home to several varieties of snake. The caves are carved from shale and pieces of rock often break off and shatter, so it's especially important to keep a keen watch. When Daddy first learned of my interest in the caves, he borrowed a few fallen trees and some vines from the woods and used them to shore up the entrances to the larger caves. Each time I come here, I give the logs a whack to make sure they're still secure. I know to look for large chunks of broken shale and to pay attention to any clumping or splits in the sod as these are signs the caves have shifted and aren't safe to enter until they've settled some. I also watch for squiggly lines in the dirt and small burrow holes; clues snakes leave behind when they're out and about. There are plenty of rattlesnakes in these parts and rattlers aren't the type to ask the same question twice.

Daddy took the gear off his back and started to unpack. My eyes went wide when I saw he'd brought his kerosene lamp along. I've never seen the caves lit up by anything but a dim flashlight. He saw me gawking at the camping lamp and grinned. A smile on my father's face is not something you see every day and I felt like I might rip out of my seams. We were on a proper adventure now.

"Hungry?" He asked, and I nodded. Battling Briarhill always leaves me hungry enough to eat three elephants and a pumpkin.

B.K. Crawford

"Fetch some firewood," he said. I did as he asked, wondering what he had in mind. A sandwich, a pickle, and a canteen of watermelon juice is what I usually bring along.

By the time I filled my arms with dry wood and returned, Daddy had the lamp lit. The mouth of the large cave glowed like nobody's business and I could barely keep inside my skin for wanting to go further in to see what I might find.

I helped Daddy stack the wood just inside the cavern rim where he said the fire would light easier, rather than out in the wind, which had started to gust. I kept looking over my shoulder to the spot where he'd placed the lamp.

"Go on," he said, "I'll make lunch."

Didn't have to ask me twice.

I studied the walls where Daddy put the lamp but I didn't see anything different, except for some sparkling rocks I hadn't noticed before. I wanted to go deeper.

"Can I move the lamp?"

"Eyawp," he answered. "Be careful and don't go too far."

The handle on the lamp already felt hot, so I took a glove out of my pack and put it on.

B.K. Crawford

About thirty feet in, I found a smooth section of wall. I put the lamp down and stepped up for a closer look. Someone had etched a series of stick figures into the stone, but the images were faint and I couldn't tell if they were old or not. For all I knew, Joey might've put them there. One of the stick figures had breasts and looked just like the ones you'd find hidden inside every boy's book cover at school. Still, I couldn't say for sure.

I heard the sound of sizzling meat and smelled burger frying. Daddy doesn't cook much, but he likes to grill and cheeseburgers are his specialty. I bet he even brought root beer because root beer and burgers are what he considers the all-American meal. My stomach grumbled, but I hushed it because I knew lunch would take a few more minutes and I wanted to see what else I might find.

I picked up the lamp and almost dropped it when a bat tore out of a hole in the wall. Then, I almost dropped it again when a sudden blast of thunder rocked the sky.

"Get back here," Daddy barked.

Happy to oblige after getting air-bombed by the bat, I scurried back.

B.K. Crawford

We ate cheeseburgers and drank our root beer while the sky opened up and spit nails. Then the storm turned mean. Lightning shot in several directions at once, zapping and cracking all around us, thunder booming like God was having trouble bringing down a seven-ten split.

When a bolt of lightning hit close by, I could feel the vibration rock my feet and it felt as though the earth might divide in two. The storm growled directly overhead. I trembled, but Daddy said hard-hitting storms never last long and besides, we had food, a fire, and the cover of the caves. I wished the noise would stop and wondered if Daddy ever heard of Noah.

The more I tried to calm down, the worse the storm got. At one point I asked Daddy if he thought the wind might form a tornado and when he didn't answer my muscles tensed to high alert. He pulled me close and we huddled by the fire, watching the flames battle the wind. After an hour or so, the ruckus eased up and we breathed easier for it.

"See?" Daddy said, "They never last long."

As soon as he said so, a God-awful explosion went off outside the cave and then,

B.K. Crawford

the mighty crack. Daddy must've sensed what happened because he jerked me back just as a giant pine fell over the mouth of the cave with a massive thud, the rush of the impact extinguishing our fire.

I felt a trickle of pee escape with my scream and Daddy cursed.

The cave started to rain shale, so Daddy shielded me beneath his broad chest and took the worst of it.

Then, everything stopped.

The sun broke through the clouds with an innocent smile, the wind turned around in search of another mountain to haunt, and the birds flapped back to their branches, ready to enjoy another day of whistle crafting.

At first glance, I thought the fallen tree had trapped us inside the cave, but areas around the lower branches allowed a tight escape. We climbed over with just enough room to squeeze through; scratches on our hands and faces the only real harm done.

The part of the tree trunk that got zapped still smoldered with smoke, blackened, and the timber had split where the lightning bolt ripped through. Pine pitch oozed from the wounds.

B.K. Crawford

"I'll bring a chainsaw up next week,"
Daddy said, reading my face as I took in the
destruction the storm had conjured. My
poor dig.

Daddy walked the length of the tree,
carefully studying it. Probably thinking about
the many things he would make with the
wood once he moved it down the mountain.
A long table, a chest of drawers and some
new shelves for his shed—I could almost hear
him thinking. When he finished, he turned to
me and said, "What do you think? You want
to head home?"

Part of me wanted to turn around and call
it a really bad day, but another part
remembered how long it took to get up the
hill. What a waste to leave without
exploring, at least a little bit.

"Sun's shining pretty good now," I
answered, not sure if he felt up for more
exploring after being pelted by shale and
ripped by pine needles.

He looked at the mess of a tree covering
the mouth of the cave. "I suppose we have
to go back inside to get our gear anyway.
Might as well have a look around."

B.K. Crawford

J. J. HOUSTON ℅120
Murder on Moon Street

Something about Joey's crystal lizard must've put Daddy in a curious mood. I admit, I felt the same way.

We crawled back over the pine and made our way inside the cave. Daddy relit the lamp and led the way as we moved deeper inside the cavern than I had ever been. I doubted Joey had ever gone so far, either. We'd stop, now and then, when something caught our fancy, but we didn't unearth anything but a few more arrowheads. That all changed when the space around us grew tight, leaving us with the choice to either go back, or wind around a sharp bend. We chose to go on.

Soon, we found ourselves at the end of the line, face-to-face with a jagged crack in the wall and, although I managed to get through it fairly quickly, Daddy had some squeezing and grunting to do. When Daddy came through with the lamp, we knew we'd stumbled onto something special.

Crystal. Everywhere. At first, I thought ice surrounded us, and it did look cold as a February fit, but we found the gems warm to the touch and smooth as glass. They grew on every inch of the walls and above us in long slender rods, pyramid shaped at the tips. Neither of us said a word for the longest

B.K. Crawford

time, just twisting and turning, watching as the light from the lamp danced off the crystals. I guessed I knew where that crystal lizard came from.

"They look like diamonds," I exclaimed. "Wouldn't it be nice if they were diamonds?"

Daddy blew a puff of air between his lips and grunted, "Lord, it would."

We took our time exploring, placing some of the more interesting crystals into my field bag. All-in-all, we spent two hours exploring.

"Gotta go," Daddy finally decided.

I blew a heavy sigh.

"It ain't going nowhere," he said. "We'll be back."

Reluctant, I nodded.

I went back through the thin crack first and waited.

The light grew brighter as Daddy approached, then it stopped. "Hold up a second," he said. Then, I heard him murmur, "What's this?" A minute or two later, he handed me the lamp and did some more squeezing and grunting until he popped through the crack.

"What'd you find?"

"Just this." He handed me a small crystal ankh. I recognized the shape from the books

B.K. Crawford

I'd read on Egyptology—a cross with a loop on top.

I squealed with delight, "It's wonderful, Daddy."

He smiled wide and ruffled my hair. "Well, there you go. Put it in your bag and let's hit the road."

On the way home, I asked when we might come back again. Daddy said it would take a few days to clear the fallen pine as he had other things to tend to as well. I felt like packing up my toothbrush and slippers. I could spend the entire summer at the caves without getting bored.

"Be patient," Daddy said, knowing it was like asking Crusher to stop scratching fleas.

B.K. Crawford

The Search For Davey Newhouse
ВЖВ

Bo saw me coming, I know he did, because he started to carry slop pails with one hand instead of two, started to spit a lot, and flexed his muscles with no real reason for it.

"Where ya been?" He looked kind of hurt, like I should have come to see him yesterday.

"Daddy wanted to go to Briarhill." I told him about the storm and the crystal cave.

"Dang-a-bang-a-lang," he spouted, adjusting the brim of his ball cap. "Be a hoot to see that."

He stared long and expectantly, waiting, I suppose, for me to offer to take him to the dig. I'd have to think about it. Bo is good in so many ways, but he has no sense for sharing. When I imagined him inside the crystal cave, there suddenly weren't any crystals left. So, I shrugged a 'maybe' and he took it in stride.

"We lost the weather vane on the barn," he pointed, "and a few weed trees. A real doozy of a storm."

I helped him with his chores and said hey to Mrs. Duke when she brought us a jug of lemonade. The whole time we were working,

B.K. Crawford

Bo kept spitting, yanking on his jeans, and flexing his muscles when I glanced in his direction. It took me some time to figure it out, but once I did, it all made sense. He must've felt I thought less of him because of the skittish way he reacted to Davey Newhouse's skeleton, so he'd commenced to demonstrating his he-manliness. What a hoot. After that, every time he spit, I'd shake my head and turn away.

When the chores were done, I told Bo about the cop lady stopping at our house after the incident at the church, about the photograph of the young boy she showed me, and why I needed to identify the boy.

He gulped lemonade from the jug and pulled his forearm across his lips when he finished, leaving a long streak of mud behind. I wondered what he looked like under all that dirt.

"The cop lady wanted to know if I'd been to the church," I confessed, and Bo's eyes went wide with horror.

"I didn't even have to lie. Daddy told her off." I swiped the jug from Bo and took a long draw. "I think she knew, though," I said, paled. "Why would she ask if she didn't see me?"

B.K. Crawford

I saw a flicker of fear in his eyes, but he just spit and nodded.

He thought about it for a minute. "If she saw you, why didn't she say so?"

"That's a right good question. I've been wondering the same."

I took a seat on a bale of hay outside the barn door. Bo sat on the bale next to me.

"Here's what we know," I said. "Someone tortured and killed Davey Newhouse in the basement of the Hornbrook house. I identified the skeleton in the coffin at the church as the same corpse I found in the basement. What we don't know is whether or not the boy in the photograph is Davey Newhouse. That's what we need to know, because if it isn't Davey, another boy has gone missing."

Bo shook his head like I'd stumped him and didn't say a word. He took his ball cap off, readjusted it, and leaned back to stare at the sky. We watched the clouds go by and named a few. After about ten minutes, Bo snapped his fingers, sat up straight and said, "My dad delivers meat to most of the folks around here. I could look and see if the Newhouse family is on his list. If they are,

B.K. Crawford

he'd have their address. Maybe we could go take a look."

"You want to bother those poor folks while they're grieving?" I was shocked at his thoughtlessness.

His face flushed with embarrassment, but he recovered quickly. "The paper said Davey had a kid sister. I bet she wouldn't mind having someone to talk to."

Not a bad idea.

B.K. Crawford

Alice Newhouse
вжв

Bo hid in the trees across the street. Now and then I heard twigs snap under his feet while he shuffled around for a better angle to keep watch. When we baked up this plan, it seemed harmless enough. But while I stood on the porch of that strange house waiting for someone to answer the door, I had second thoughts.

At least two sizes too small, the scout troop uniform I wore once belonged to my sister, Jackie, and it smelled of moth balls after spending the last eight years stuffed in a box in the attic. Worse, Bo didn't do a very good job of repacking the wrapper on the half full box of cookies I held in my hand. I had phony written all over me.

I pressed my hands over the cotton material, trying to iron out the wrinkles in the dress.

If there's one thing I can't stand, it's girlie clothes. Wearing a dress automatically means no play, no fun, no adventure. You can't get a dress dirty or hissy fits abound. It's like being benched. I wore a pair of cutoff shorts under the uniform, but somehow they

B.K. Crawford

didn't help. My legs still felt exposed and vulnerable.

Turned out Mr. Duke did deliver meat to the Newhouse family and Bo had no trouble finding their address in the records. Unfortunately, we had to walk a couple miles to their place; me in a dress and Bo chuckling beside me.

Naturally, Bo came up with the harebrained idea for the disguise.   We would put the uniform in my field bag, I'd change in the woods down the road a piece, and go to the Newhouse place where we hoped Davey's sister would answer the door.

When I changed into the dress, Bo laughed, whistled, and said he wouldn't mind seeing me in a wedding gown. I told him right then and there I would never marry him unless he also wore a frilly dress. That shut him up. But, I felt like I'd lost my nerve and told him we should abandon the scheme and go home.

Bo insisted the worst that could happen was nobody would buy the cookies and if they did, we'd make a nice profit seeing as how the box was only half full. I didn't like the idea of cheating anybody out of their hard-earned money, so I told him I wouldn't

do it unless he put fifty-cents inside the box.
Boy, oh boy, he looked like I'd sucked his soul
out through his nose with a straw, but he
finally agreed to do it.

 I noticed the fancy paved driveway first
thing when we arrived at the house. Second
thing, no car parked there. But, that didn't
mean anything. Lots of houses have garages
out back where you can't see them. I
stepped onto the porch, knocked on the door
and thought to turn around and go back the
way I came. Especially when I realized I
hadn't changed out of my high-top sneakers.
I couldn't say what a bona fide troop member
wears on her feet, I was only four when my
sister got her last badge, but I'd bet chewed
up high-tops weren't part of the dress code.

 I knocked on the door again and noticed a
small white button on the door frame. I
pushed it and heard the muffled sound of a
bell ringing inside. Yep, these people were
rich. They even had paint on the house—a
nice sky blue. A wide swing on the porch
looked big enough to seat three, and loads of
brightly colored potted flowers surrounded
the swing. Very pretty.

 I felt sure no one would answer the door.

B.K. Crawford

I turned around to look into the trees across the street where Bo hid and shrugged my shoulders in defeat. Just then, I heard a small voice call from the other side of the door, "Who's there?"

"I'm selling cookies," I stammered.

The door opened a crack and a freckled face peeked around the edge of the door.

"Are they chocolate?"

My heart skipped a beat. Davey Newhouse's sister. I read the label on the package in my hand.

"Chocolate caramel. My last box."

"I can't let you in. My parents aren't home."

I said I understood.

"How much for the cookies?"

"Um. A dollar?"

She opened the door a little wider and looked me over, head to toe. She furled her brow and seemed irritated with me. Maybe I'd asked for too much money. What do I know about selling cookies? I turned to go and waved good-bye, thinking it a shame to get so close and come away with nothing.

"Wait. I know you," she blurted. "Aren't you the girl who got thrown off the bus for clocking Arty Schmidt in the eye?"

B.K. Crawford

I felt my face flush, but I nodded and told her my name.

She opened the door wide.

"I'm Alice." She grabbed me by the arm and swept me into the foyer. "That rotten snot ball has yanked every pony tail in school," she bellyached.

I smiled. That's exactly why I popped him one.

The next thing you know, I'm sitting on a fat, white sofa, drinking soda pop and eating cookies with Alice Newhouse, complaining about schoolyard bullies. For the longest time, I forgot why I'd come.

Alice ate the last cookie and washed it down with a swig of soda pop.

"So, why are you really here?" She burped. Leaning close, she twirled a cherry colored curl around her finger and studied me like bacteria on a test strip.

I raised my eyebrows in surprise and tried to think of something to say.

"I don't think you want to be my friend. I'm younger than you and crossing that line is pretty much forbidden, isn't it?"

She leaned closer. I got nervous. Her green eyes looked puffy. I supposed she'd

B.K. Crawford

done her share of crying over the past few days.

Just a little thing and made up like an oversized doll, she wore a bow in her hair, dress starched, shoes shiny, and yet, she held a hard expression on her face. Was it heartache or general meanness? I felt uneasy.

"I just... I... I just thought...maybe... I wondered if..."

"What?"

"Could I see a picture of your brother?" I finally spit out.

"Davey? You're not here to see me?" She groaned and looked hurt. I thought I might understand. I spent a good portion of my life overshadowed by five older brothers and sisters, although none of them had died. I figured the past few days had revolved around Davey and his funeral, leaving very little time or attention for Alice. Life is rough when you feel invisible. So, I told her I thought she was a load of fun and her expression softened.

"It's really, really important," I pleaded.

"But," she protested, "You've seen Davey before. On the bus."

B.K. Crawford

"I'm sure I have. I just can't remember.
It's like you said, I ignored the younger kids.
I've tried and tried, but I don't remember his
face."

"Why's it so important? You know he
died, right? We just had his funeral." Her
voice shattered as she spoke and I felt like an
intruder. I didn't belong there, standing in
the way of her grief. Especially if the casket
we knocked over at the church held her
brother's remains.

I nodded and struggled with how much I
should tell her. "I'm so sorry. It's just
that...well... Here, look."

I handed her the threatening letter I'd
gotten in the mail. When she read it, her
eyes popped and she thrust the letter back at
me, like it might grow teeth and bite her.

"What's that got to do with Davey?"

"Honestly, I can't be sure until I see his
face."

She stood up, moved to the fireplace, and
pointed at a portrait hanging over the
mantle.

"That's us. We're twins."

Huge, the picture hung in plain view for
half an hour or more and I didn't even notice
it. Some detective.

B.K. Crawford

Confused, I gawked at Davey's gap-toothed smile. Definitely the boy in the photograph Lieutenant Shafer showed me and the corpse Joey and I found hanging in the Hornbrook basement. So, why did the Lieutenant ask me about him when she already knew he'd died? And, the questions she'd asked: Did I know him? Did I talk to him? Did he ever tell me anything scary? What were they about?

"Alice, when was the last time you saw Davey?"

"He went off to school in September last year."

"School? Around here?"

"No, a military cadet place. Forest Ledge Academy, I think. I cried. It hurts something awful when we're separated. Unless you have a twin, you can't really understand."

"Didn't he call? Or write?"

She shook her head and tears welled up in her eyes. "I never got a letter, but I know he would've written if they let him. He hurts, too, when we're separated. Mom and Dad said he called every Saturday night, but after I was asleep. I begged them to let me call, but they said the cadets couldn't accept phone calls." Alice sobbed, hiding her face in

B.K. Crawford

her hands, her shoulders rocking with sorrow.

I rubbed her back and gave her time to recover.

"I know it's really, really hard to talk about, but I wonder... No, maybe I shouldn't ask."

"It's okay." She wiped her eyes. "You can ask."

"No, I shouldn't. I should go. I'm so very, very sorry for your loss, Alice. Thank you for everything."

"Really, I don't mind. You can stay a minute longer and ask whatever you want."

I felt awkward and unsure, but finally found the courage to ask, "How did Davey die?"

She sat on the couch and hugged a pillow. "A riding accident. He fell off a horse and broke his neck."

"When?"

Her voice faded, "Last week."

I heard Bo running through the woods as I made my way down the hill. He came out of cover after I turned a bend in the road. Breathless, he ran to join me.

"Was it him?"

I nodded. Alice's story shook me to the middle and I felt so sorry for her. Her parents

B.K. Crawford

definitely lied about receiving phone calls from Davey. It had been weeks since Joey and I found the corpse and it sure looked like Davey had already hung there for a long time before we discovered him. No way did he die only a week ago and I doubted he broke his neck, at least not until Bo dumped him on the church floor. Why would Alice's parents lie? To spare Alice the heartache? Or, maybe they weren't sure Davey was dead. Maybe someone blackmailed them and they were hoping to get him back alive. My head swam with the possibilities.

Maybe I read too many detective stories. I always wondered what it was like to get caught up in a real-life mystery. It's no fun at all.

B.K. Crawford

Off To See The Wizard
ВЖВ

The following day, Miss Tilly used paperclips to fasten an elastic chin strap to the toilet plunger. I tried to squirm out of it, but she ultimately won the battle and placed it on my head. Apparently, the wicked witch of the west swiped Miss Tilly's infamous barbeque sauce recipe and she intended to get it back. With the plunger in place, I became the Tin man, who, as I understood it, Miss Tilly would task with contacting the Lion who, in turn, would go after the witch and retrieve the recipe. Miss Tilly rigged more elastic to two small parasol umbrellas and tied them onto each of her outer thighs. She opened the umbrellas and covered them with her over-sized skirt. Glittering wand in hand, she became the wide-hipped Glinda, good witch of the north.

If I hadn't seen Miss Tilly prepare her barbeque sauce on several occasions, I might have sat there for an entire week waiting for the cowardly Lion to rescue the recipe. As it was, it took an hour to play along as I recited the ingredients slowly, claiming the Lion had done a good job of torturing the information

B.K. Crawford

out of the witch. In the end, Miss Tilly seemed satisfied with the results and allowed me to remove the plunger from my head. With the card safely returned to her recipe box, she put the wand down, removed the awkward umbrellas and made tea.

I finally had my opportunity to ask about Mr. Newhouse.

"He works for the state," she said. "Travels between the capitol and Washington, D.C., with Hank Hornbrook in tow most of the time."

My heart skipped a beat when she mentioned Hornbrook, but I did my best to stay calm and act casual.

"Hank Hornbrook. Is he the one who owns the Hornbrook house?"

She nodded.

"He works for the government, too?"

"Sure. He's not as high up as Carl Newhouse. He's just a helper. What do they call the peons?" She thought about it for a second, then lifted a finger, "An aide."

She asked why I wanted to know and I waved it off as unimportant, saying I'd met Alice and what a sweet girl she was. Miss Tilly smiled and said, "How nice. It's good for a young girl to have lady friends. You shouldn't spend all your time in the company of muddy boys." I raised my eyebrows at that, wondering if she knew how much time I spent with Bo.

Like I said before, for a woman who rarely leaves her house, she still manages to know more about what's going on than anyone else in the neighborhood.

"There's another one missing, you know," she said, sipping her tea.

"A recipe?" I sank down in my chair, dreading another hour with the toilet plunger stuck to my head.

"No. Another boy. Seven years old, from nearby. No one's talking about it though and it doesn't look like anyone is in a hurry to find him."

"Then, how do you know?"

"How do I know what?"

"How do you know he's missing? If no one's talking about it?"

She puckered her lips in a playful way and flashed her eyes. "I have my ways."

Why would she tell me about missing children? Did she know I'd searched for clues? It seemed to me she'd have a royal fit if she did. But, she didn't just say a boy had gone missing, she said *another* boy had gone

B.K. Crawford

missing, which meant she knew about Davey Newhouse and she knew I knew. I couldn't escape the feeling that somehow Miss Tilly was hip to everything I'd learned and more.

When we finished our tea, she put the cups in the sink and disappeared for a minute. She came back with a fresh roll of toilet paper and handed it to me.

"Ask Mr. Charles why he took my needlepoint."

I sighed and headed for the outhouse.

"Tell him I've had it up to here with his shenanigans," she yelled.

I remembered seeing the needlepoint sitting on the hamper in the bathroom when I went to tinkle earlier, so when I came back from the outhouse I told Miss Tilly, "Pappy says it's not sanitary to sew in the bathroom. Oh, and he said muddy boys aren't all bad."

She looked taken aback for a second, then gently swatted me on the arm. "Who do you want to take advice from? Me, or a man who uses twelve pair of underwear for a brain?"

I gave her a kiss good-bye and went home to wash my hair.

The air felt feverish and by the time I got home I'd worked up a sweat from the bike ride, so I put on a bathing suit, grabbed a

B.K. Crawford

bottle of shampoo, and went for a swim in the creek. Like always, the cold water raised goosebumps on my skin. Once my body adjusted to the temperature, I washed and rinsed my hair, watched the soap suds disappear downstream, then wrapped an arm around my favorite rock and let my feet float, toes up. I thought about what I'd learned from Miss Tilly while the brisk current massaged me.

I had finally uncovered my first connection in the case. Mr. Newhouse and Hank Hornbrook worked together. Was it a coincidence Davey Newhouse ended up dead in Hornbooks' basement? I doubted it. In fact, it seemed all the world to me that Hank Hornbrook had probably killed Davey. Rusty luck, though, the cops didn't see Davey hanging there, only Joey and I had, and they didn't believe us. Because of that, they wouldn't make the connection. I'd have to find another link and, to do that, I needed to know more. As much as I didn't like the idea, I decided I needed to visit Phoebe Hornbrook again. Hopefully, she'd had her fill of little girl stew.

B.K. Crawford

J. J. HOUSTON ℅142
Murder on Moon Street

Momma made her famous lasagna for dinner. The house smelled so good, I drooled the whole time it took me to change into dry clothes. Momma reminded me not to eat too much because lasagna tends to upset my stomach and she put extra salad and peas on my plate to make up the difference. Crusher whined under the table while we ate. I imagine the aroma drove him nuts, but he gets even sicker than I do on tomato sauce. I ate more than I should have, but I went slow and finished off the peas to boot. Grateful for such a scrumptious meal, I washed the dishes without anyone having to ask.

I went to bed content and fell off to sleep like a baby in a padded cradle.

The extra lasagna caught up with me around two o'clock in the morning when I awoke with terrible stomach cramps. I noticed the time because the clock on my bedside table was lit up like the face of a full moon. In an awful hurry, I made my way downstairs and spent the next hour groaning on the toilet. As my trouble began to ease, I wondered about the clock.

Momma keeps heavy drapes on the windows in my room even in the summer because we can't afford to switch them out

B.K. Crawford

every time the seasons change. I remembered closing the drapes before I went to bed. So, how could I have seen the clock so well when I woke up? Had someone come into my room and opened the drapes? That thought scared me plenty. What if Hank Hornbrook had come to do me in? I almost screamed for Daddy, but realized, if Hank Hornbrook broke into our house, I'd probably already be dead. Wouldn't I?

My cramps got worse and the smell would have put a bull in a stumbling daze. I worried until I had nothing left to squirt, then flushed, washed my hands, and tiptoed up the stairs.

Wide eyed and holding my breath, I peeked around the door frame. The drapes were still closed. The air trapped inside my lungs spilled out all at once.

I hadn't noticed when I first awoke, thanks to the stomach pain, but a strange blue hue radiated inside my room. No wonder I could read the clock. What caused that light and where did it come from?

I pulled the string connected to the light fixture in the ceiling, but when the light came on it smothered the eerie glow, so I turned it back off, allowing the curious illumination to return. As my eyesight adjusted, my focus

B.K. Crawford

fell beneath the bed where the glimmer seemed brightest. Bending down, I peered under the bunk. Swatting my sneakers out of the way, I gasped when I saw my field bag yawning an eerie blue glow. Grabbing the strap, I dragged the bag out and found the crystal ankh pulsating inside, inhaling and exhaling light. I never saw anything so strange. Mesmerized, I watched, not quite sure what to make of it. It looked alive. For the second time in an hour, I thought about waking Daddy. I mulled it over, changing my mind at least a dozen times. I felt sure the ankh wouldn't do anything but glow and since it didn't seem to pose a danger, it might be best to let Daddy get a good night's sleep.

Our coffee percolator makes funny sounds. *Puh-puh-puh-puuuuuuh, puh-puh-puh-puuuuuuh*—it goes on like a tiny train engine until it's finished, then it sounds like it might up and die. Daddy and I sat at the kitchen table waiting for the brew to finish, the small bulb over the sink giving off a dim yellow light. He rubbed his eyes between glares. He always spits nails when I wake him up at three-thirty in the morning. I hoped the coffee would help.

B.K. Crawford

Murder on Moon Street

"What is wrong with you?" His tone suggested I might have a screw loose.

He put some milk in his coffee and I gave him the chance to drink a few sips. Then I warned him, saying I had something surprising. I turned the light off over the sink, opened the field bag and let the glow escape. He spit a mouthful of coffee and some of it splattered on my face and chest, not hot enough to burn. Jumping to his feet, Daddy jerked the bag out of my arms. I suppose he thought something dangerous lurked inside. That's the reason I decided to wake him up after all; I just couldn't convince myself of the ankh's safety.

Daddy peered into the bag. "It's that thing I found in the cave," he gasped.

I nodded.

He grabbed a pair of garden gloves off a shelf on the back porch and put them on. Reaching into the bag, he removed the ankh and watched it, fascinated with the way it seemed to breathe.

He set it on the table and stared. Once his initial fear passed, he seemed downright giddy, chuckling and mumbling. He must've said, "Would ya look at that?" at least ten times and even smiled a time or two.

B.K. Crawford

"You don't think it might be radioactive?" I asked, sheepishly.

He shook his head like the thought didn't concern him and I breathed easier for it.

"Where's that lizard?" He asked, and I had to think about where I'd left it.

"Upstairs. In my dresser drawer."

"Go get it."

I pounded up the stairs until I remembered Momma was still asleep, then I tiptoed the rest of the way.

I don't expect anyone to believe what happened next. Heck, I can't lay claim to believing it myself.

I found the crystal lizard in the drawer where I left it, so I snatched it and took it to Daddy. He set it down on the table near the ankh and it started to glow green. Once it got a good glow going, the hocus-pocus began.

It started with a soft hum, so low, I had to strain to hear it, then the two pieces vibrated ever so slightly. After that, they started talking to each other. They sounded like chirping crickets, the lizard the more excited of the two. Their vibration increased and both pieces glowed even brighter. After a minute of that, the ankh lifted off the table

B.K. Crawford

about ten inches or so, and just hovered there, happy as a clam on a cloud.

Daddy and I both sat there with our jaws unhinged, staring in awe. Then Momma turned the lights on. The crystals lost their glow and the ankh fell onto the table with a thud.

Bleary-eyed, Momma patted her hair and said, "What are you two doing?"

We didn't tell her.

B.K. Crawford

The Vanishing Act

ВЖВ

Carnivals in these parts give people a reason to live. Unless you're fascinated by watching the grass grow, or particular to sniffing cow fumes, there isn't much excitement out our way. So, when the county carnival rolls into town once a year, everyone gears up for a party. Momma gets to visit with some of her lady friends and Daddy sits in the beer tent throwing the suds back all night. Normally, I tag along, clinging to Momma's skirt, but this year she said it's all right if I go with Bo and his folks.

The carnival set up two days early because the weatherman called for thunderstorms over the weekend. Daddy says being a weatherman is the job to have because they get paid for being wrong all the time. I didn't care if they were right or wrong. Early to the carnival is better than late, or not at all.

Mr. Duke pulled into the parking lot as the sky turned a field lily orange. A truck pulled in next to us and seven boys jumped off the flatbed, whooping and hollering. Some of the carnival booths already had their festive lights on, twinkling out an invitation to come

B.K. Crawford

play their games. Bo and I breathed deep.
The smell of popcorn, cotton candy, hot dogs
and hamburgers, sausage sandwiches, candy
apples and funnel cakes filled us with desire.

Bo's parents told us to meet them at the
entrance gate in three hours and let us go
our own way. As soon as they were out of
sight, Bo tried to hold my hand. I pulled
away, even though he looked real nice. All
cleaned up, he shined like a new nickel and
I'd never seen him like that before. In fact, I
didn't even know he had blonde hair. My
rejection didn't seem to rattle him much, he
just smiled, shoved his hands in his pockets
and asked what I wanted to do. Like I knew.

Daddy never had money to blow on games
and he claims they're rigged anyway, so, in
the past, I'd just walk around and watch
everyone else have fun. I didn't expect Bo to
spend his money on me, he ain't the type,
and I made peace with that a long time ago.
Just being on the fairway sent a thrill up my
spine.

We walked around, listening to carousel
music, watching people toss rings at bottles,
throw darts at balloons, and shoot BB guns at
metal ducks. What a hoot.

B.K. Crawford

An announcer came over the loud speaker to say the tractor pull contest would start in a few minutes, so Bo and I headed in that direction.

If you've never been to a tractor pull before, it goes like this: Some of the local farmers trick out their tractors with monster engines and compete to see which one can pull the most weight through a muddy field. The winner gets a cash prize.

By the time the contest finished, my eardrums were numb from the roar of the engines and the screaming crowd.

After the pull, we left the field and went back to the main drag. The sun slipped below the horizon and I told Bo I felt chilly. He asked why I didn't bring a jacket. It never occurred to him to offer me his. See what I mean?

He leaned in close and I thought he might try to kiss me, but, instead, he whispered something in my ear. I couldn't hear what he said over the carousel music. He spoke up a bit and said, "Someone's following us. Don't look."

I looked.

"Where?"

B.K. Crawford

He threw his shoulder into mine and said, "Keep walking."

We walked around the grounds twice and every now and then, I caught a glimpse of an old fellow wearing a dark suit. He looked out of place at a farmer's carnival and when he caught me looking, he'd duck behind a booth or get lost in the crowd. I couldn't help but wonder if it might be Hank Hornbrook.

Bo decided we could lose him by going into the tunnel of love. I complained, saying we could do the same by riding the Ferris wheel, or the roller coaster, or even the haunted house, but Bo insisted on the tunnel of love. He shocked me by offering to pay for the ride. Why would I argue?

The line for the ride stretched around the corner, so we waited almost ten minutes.

We picked a boat decorated like an Egyptian barge, trimmed in blue and gold. We stepped inside and the ride attendant hooked our seatbelts for us. Bo's smile reached from ear to ear. Again, he tried to take my hand. Again, I refused.

The ride began outside, but a motorized rope winch slowly pulled the boat into the mouth of a dark tunnel. As soon as we entered the passageway, Bo started to shake

B.K. Crawford

the boat, probably trying to scare me into his arms, but I told him to quit it. He settled down and we moved on.

I'd never been on a carnival ride before and I intended to soak it all in. The lights ahead of us swayed dim and mesmerizing. Colorful scenery painted on the walls set the mood—white swans and pink roses, cupids and their fated arrows, all serenaded by dreamy music.

There's always a trick with carnivals, though, as Daddy likes to point out. Carnies are masters at making loads of money by giving little to nothing in return. The ride only lasted two minutes. Naturally, I felt the desire to start all over and do it again. That's how they rake in the dough.

Although I expected more advances, Bo remained the perfect gentleman the entire time. When the boat slipped out of the tunnel and our short ride came to an end, I realized why Bo had behaved so well.

He wasn't in the boat.

Frantic, I ran back to the ride entrance and screamed until I caught the attention of the attendant. I told him Bo fell out of the boat. He asked which boat we were in and I pointed to the Egyptian one. He told me to stay put while he took a flashlight inside to check the waterway. It seemed to take him forever to get back to me. When he arrived, he said he didn't find anyone in the water. I felt some relief at that—at least Bo hadn't drowned. Then the attendant inspected the boat and, with a look of shock pasted on his face, said someone had sliced Bo's seatbelt with a knife. Panic took me.

My thoughts circled back to the man who'd followed us. I ran through the grounds, bumping into people, not stopping to say I'm sorry, looking for Daddy, or Mr. Duke, anyone who might help me find Bo.

I raced to the beer tent, scanning the crowd for Daddy's face. I wondered how I would explain Bo's disappearance. Would Daddy want to know why someone would follow me and Bo, or would the shock of Bo's disappearance keep him focused on the search? Sooner or later he would want the whole story. Honestly, if I had to, I'd confess. I just wanted to find Bo before he ended up in a cowboy costume. The thought haunted me through-and-through.

I couldn't find Daddy anywhere. On a hunch, I ran back toward the tunnel of love, hoping to see a familiar face along the way. Where had everyone gone?

When I arrived at the tunnel, I crossed over a twisted nest of heavy-duty electric cables and made my way through a narrow alley that allowed access to the rear of the ride. If Bo hadn't left the carnival grounds, he had to be here somewhere. Not a single light bulb burned behind the fairway so I stood there waiting for my eyes to adjust to the deep darkness.

I heard a moan and twisted toward the sound but couldn't see much more than shadows and shape lines.

"Bo?" I thought I heard another moan.

The cables beneath my feet felt thick as rattle snakes; one wrong move and I would either trip, unplug something, or get zapped.

"Bo? Where are you?" No reply.

Still frantic, I imagined him lying on the ground, bleeding, dying of a mortal wound. I blamed myself for getting him into this mess.

Cautiously, I moved through the darkness, calling Bo's name, straining to listen for a response over the blaring carnival noise.

I felt someone grab me from behind.

The punch landed before I even realized I'd made a fist. A carnie came around the

B.K. Crawford

corner, sporting a massive flashlight. Only then did I see Bo in the sawdust, his hands cupping a bloody nose. My stomach felt like it jumped off a cliff.

"Stop beating on me, woman," Bo screeched, after I helped him to his feet. Lord, I couldn't have felt worse if a herd of elephants used my head as a trampoline.

I hugged him. Hard.

"I was so scared," I gushed.

"Not supposed to be back here," the carnie growled, motioning for us to get out.

Bo pulled a handkerchief from his pocket and tended to his nose, then he took me by the hand and I let him. We returned to the fairway where I could see the sawdust in his hair and his swollen nose. Shiner in the morning, for sure.

Bo led me toward the entrance gate, away from the loud music.

"What happened?" I panted.

"Someone nabbed me off the boat right after we moved into the tunnel. I heard you say quit it, but I couldn't answer because he had his hand over my mouth. He popped me in the head with something hard and threw a burlap bag over my face. There's a dummy wall near the back of the building. I'm

B.K. Crawford

guessing that's how he got in. He dragged me through there, with my arms locked behind my back. Otherwise, I could've taken him, you know I could. Then he says if me and my girlfriend don't mind our own business, he'll make sure we both wind up in his rodeo. Then he left. I guess I passed out from the woozy."

My heartbeat increased a hundred beats with every word Bo spoke.

"He said that?"

Bo nodded. "Yep, called you my girlfriend."

"No, not that. He said we'd wind up in his rodeo?"

Bo caressed his nose with his fingertips and nodded again.

"Cowboys ride in rodeos," I mumbled.

B.K. Crawford

Guilt-Ridden

BЖB

Farm boys know how to use guilt to get what they want.

The morning after the carnival, I went to see Bo's shiner. He looked like a rabid raccoon, the skin around his eyes blackened, purple and puffy. I felt so responsible and would've given almost anything to see him looking as nice as he did before the carnival. I'm sure he sensed my guilt because I ended up cooking and serving him a second breakfast. Mrs. Duke had already given him eggs and toast, but he said he had a hankering for Canadian bacon and homegrown sausage. So, I gave in and plopped a frying pan on the stove.

While he ate, I asked him how he explained his injuries to his parents.

"Told them the truth. Told them you clocked me one."

"Oh, jeez, Bo. They probably hate me."

He shook his head. "Nah, I said I tried to get fresh and you were only defending yourself."

"Well, now they probably think their little boy is a pervert," I giggled.

B.K. Crawford

He grunted and hoisted a glass of orange juice to his lips. Every swallow hurt, I could tell by the way he winced.

"I almost told them," he said.

"Told them what?"

"About the trouble you're in. About the man at the carnival."

"Why didn't you?"

"Because after last night, I want to see him hang as bad as you do. I reckon you're right about him getting away unless we find some evidence, so evidence is what we'll get. You don't mess with Beauregard Dexter Duke and walk away without a bite mark on your ass."

I laughed, partly at his macho man bravado, but mostly at his name.

He finished his food, grabbed an ice pack out of the freezer and sat there looking pitiful as can be. He's so overgrown and rugged most of the time, it's easy to forget he's only a kid, except for the helpless expression on his face.

"What can I do to make it better, Bo?"

Sitting up straight and looking suddenly stronger, he answered without missing a beat.

"Take me to the caves."

I scowled.

B.K. Crawford

"Come on. Have pity on a broken man."
He flashed his sad puppy eyes.

"Broken men need to stay home and
heal," I gently coaxed.

I knew I shouldn't have told him about the
glowing lizard and the levitating ankh, but
aside from Miss Tilly, I don't have anyone
else to confide in. Bo is my best friend. But, I
still felt like he'd rob the cave blind if I took
him there.

He pouted. When that didn't work, he
pouted some more. I refused to give in.
Then, he leaned over and mumbled, "Did you
know the earth moves at sixty-five thousand
miles an hour through space? If a man sits
still too long, he might get dizzy."

I raised my eyebrows. "Really? How do
you know that?"

He blew a puff of air through his lips.
"What? I read, too, ya know."

"I didn't know you thought about scientific
things."

"One of these days you might take some
time to get to know me," he pouted.

"Bo, we grew up together."

"I got news for ya, Honey Pie. People
change. Besides, growing up with someone

B.K. Crawford

doesn't mean you know squat. Sometimes, it's an excuse to skip the knowing."

I sat back in my chair and folded my arms across my chest. "Look at you, a budding philosopher."

Beaming, he nodded. "I'm full of surprises."

I agreed to take Bo to the dig site if he would go with me to visit Phoebe Hornbrook. If Hank Hornbrook had bopped Bo in the head at the carnival, as we suspected, then maybe Phoebe could give us some useful information on his character. Bo took the deal on a pinky swear.

B.K. Crawford

A Long Fall

ВЖВ

Two and a half hours later we stood at the dig site.

We stopped by my place first to pack a lunch and get my tools. Daddy gave his camping lamp to Bo and told us to be careful because he didn't have a chance to remove the fallen pine yet. I made a solemn promise and off we went.

We ate our peanut butter and jelly sandwiches at Copper pond. There, I told Bo about Gachoo, the water monster. He laughed and poked fun at me for being so gullible, but when a splash erupted in the middle of the pond, Bo leapt to his feet and seemed in an awful hurry to get going. I'd seen the small fish jump but didn't tell him.

Once we got to the site, we climbed through the tree branches of the fallen pine without too much trouble, just a scrape on my arm and a small tear in Bo's jeans. We lit the lamp inside the large cavern and I led the way as we snaked around the bend leading to the crystal cave. Bo didn't say a word as the walls thinned and we arrived at the crack. I put down the lamp.

B.K. Crawford

"You promised not to take anything out of here without my say so," I reminded him.

"Scouts honor," he nodded.

"You're not a scout."

"C'mon, J.J., I want to see. Let's go."

"I want your word."

He held his hands up like I'd put him under arrest. "Alright, alright, I promise."

I went through the crack first and had him hand me the lamp, then he squeezed through and expelled a loud gasp.

"Holy Jiminy, it's just like Superman's fortress of solitude. You read the comics, right?" He turned toward me, his face beaming with awe. I suppose I must have worn the same expression when I first saw the crystals.

Bo twisted and turned, taking it all in.

"How long you figure this place has been here? Right under our noses and nobody knowing a thing about it," he gushed.

"Millions of years," I assumed.

"Dang-a-bang-a-lang," he breathed, moving to pet a nearby crystal like a kitten.

I put the lamp on a level stone and told Bo to go ahead and explore, reminding him we were looking for more artifacts like the ankh and lizard.

B.K. Crawford

"I'm gonna check your pockets before we leave," I warned.

"Trust is the foundation for a good relationship. You'll have to work on that before we get married," he razzed, moving out of the way so my slap missed him by a few inches.

"Seriously, Bo. If you find anything strange, tell me."

"Roger that."

Most archeologists carry field brushes in their kits, but since I couldn't afford a proper kit, Miss Tilly gave me a whisk brush I could use for unearthing artifacts without damaging them. After the menacing bear on Briarhill Trail stole that one, Bo gave me another. I took the brush out of my pack and started dusting around the floor. Now and then I'd hear Bo grunt as he climbed through the tangled crystal web that must have seemed like a jungle gym to him. He'd already made it halfway to the top of the cavern, but since I didn't think he could hurt anything, I held my tongue and focused on the task at hand.

About an hour into the dig, I found a scarab beetle fashioned entirely out of crystal, just like the ankh and the lizard. I

B.K. Crawford

brushed off the dirt and debris and yelled for Bo to come see. I heard his grunts as he squirreled back toward me.

"Almost there," he said a few times, then went back to panting.

I picked up the lamp and moved it closer to the crystal labyrinth that posed above me like a glass spider web with Bo in its grasp. I could tell by his groaning he slithered high above my head and had a way to go before he came through.

While I waited, I inspected the beetle. It filled the palm of my hand, smooth as ice. The detail carved into the crystal made it seem as though it might come alive if only I knew how to activate it. I wondered if it could glow like the ankh and the lizard.

"Almost there," Bo said again, close this time. I could see him squirming through the last shards. He lost his footing and squealed. My stomach turned. If he fell from that high up, he wouldn't walk away without breaking a bone. Somehow he managed to catch himself, dangling from a shard almost as thick as his own body. With his arms wrapped tightly around, he clung to the crystal.

"You can't jump," I warned. "It's too high. Go back and find another way."

B.K. Crawford

He looked at me, his face purple with the effort it took to hold on. He tried to smile, but I could see the terror in his eyes.

"Go back up."

He nodded and started to swing his leg, trying to reach an adjacent crystal, but kept coming up short. We both heard the snapping, like the sound of icicles shattering, only much louder. Bo scrambled, frantic to get off the shard. He looked like a Saturday morning cartoon character as his legs flailed, trying to run in midair with nothing for a foothold. The more he squirmed, the more the shard creaked in protest.

"It's gonna break. Use your arms."

He relaxed his legs and began to pull himself up, hand-over-hand, slowly scaling the shard. I held my breath. Every time he moved, the shard groaned another warning. He kept stopping to look down at me, as if I had a magic wand stuffed in my pocket. I didn't. I could only watch, pray, and offer a little encouragement.

"Don't stop. Just a little more. You can make it."

He looked at the shard he hoped to reach, then gave me one last look of desperation. Taking a deep breath, he clambered as fast as

B.K. Crawford

his arms would allow. When he got to the tip, the shard made a final complaint as it shattered from the inside out, raining debris with the explosion. I shielded my eyes with my arms and prayed Bo hadn't fallen. I couldn't hear him over the noise of the shattering crystal and couldn't see him with my eyes covered.

I waited for the clatter to stop and screamed for him.

"That was close," he twittered from high up in the web of glass.

Thank God.

"You could've killed us both, you nitwit." I yelled. "Get down here and, for crying out loud, come the safe way."

It took him twenty minutes to navigate the crystal maze. Finally, he stood next to me.

"Where's your beetle?" He asked.

Of course I'd lost it when the shard exploded.

"I dropped it. Help me find it."

Finding a sugar molecule named Mike in a glass of chocolate milk would have been easier than locating the beetle among a pile of broken crystal. The edges on some of the shards were sharp as razors, so I put my gloves on and gave a pair to Bo. We

B.K. Crawford

searched where I'd stood during the collapse, but I couldn't say if the beetle had flown out of my hand when the explosion startled me, or if it had gotten kicked around by falling debris afterward.

While we searched, I repeatedly thanked God for two things—for Bo's safety and for not taking our lamp away. Stubborn, I stayed in the area where I'd stood during the excitement while Bo scoured a wider perimeter. The boy made me nervous. Why couldn't he stay close by, especially after what just happened? I didn't complain, though, because I wanted the beetle and I knew it could be anywhere after the commotion. I continued my search, hoping Bo didn't have any more disaster cards stuffed up his sleeve.

Half an hour later, after hearing nothing but the crunch of glass under foot, Bo piped up, "What say whoever finds the beetle gets a big kiss? A little competition. How about it?"

I stood up, wiped crystal dust off my knees and went to him. "Give it to me."

He blushed, handed me the beetle and leaned against a stalagmite in defeat. I hardly had time to wonder why a single

B.K. Crawford

stalagmite would grow in a crystal cave when we both felt the ground begin to tremble beneath our feet. Before we could move, the ground opened and swallowed us both.

We filled the seemingly endless fall with a lot of screaming on both our parts, though it's true Bo sounds a lot more like a girl than I do. We fell through the unending hole, squirming, and I felt sure death awaited us at the bottom, if we ever reached bottom. We had more than enough time to consider the mistakes of the day many times over as we slipped through the darkness. I thought about the promise I'd made to Daddy about being careful—so much for that—and I thought about Miss Tilly. Who would act out her fantasies with her if I died? I thought about Davey Newhouse's murder. Who would find evidence against Mr. Hornbrook now? I thought about my brothers and sisters, scattered across the globe. Who would write them funny letters? Then I thought about Joey, stuck in the mountains with a gaggle of girls for the rest of the summer. I tried, but really couldn't find any remorse. He'd asked for it. I thought about all of that while Bo continued to scream like it made a difference. I didn't think any less of

B.K. Crawford

him. It seemed the normal thing to do under the circumstances. But, the same calm that came over me when I got caught in the woods with the bear had returned. My life would end in a massive hole in the ground and no one could do anything about it. It's part of the risk a good archeologist takes. But, I felt bad for Bo. If I hadn't brought him to the cave, he might've lived to see another sunrise. That single regret wrapped around my soul like a cocoon and I allowed it to blanket me.

A light appeared below us, dim and approaching quickly. I sensed that wherever this hole led, we were about to make an untidy arrival. I couldn't remember the words to the Lord's prayer—something about the shadow of death. I saw a floor shining like metal, but smooth like glass. We were coming in too fast. The shadow of death. I tucked my head into my arms and closed my eyes tight. Bo's scream grew louder. Then a hissing sound erupted, like a thousand people blowing air through their lips all at once.

Our descent slowed until it stopped altogether, leaving us both hovering inches

B.K. Crawford

off the floor. It felt as if someone with very large hands had reached out to catch us.

Safe, but Lord knows how many miles beneath the surface of the Earth.

'Yea, though I walk through the valley of the shadow of death, I shall fear no evil.'

When the hissing stopped altogether, Bo and I stood with our feet planted firmly on the ground, staring at each other in a daze. Bo spoke first, "Where's my granddaddy? He's supposed to take me to see Jesus."

"We're not dead."

"Yes we are. No one falls that far and lives. You're in shock. Get over it, ghosts are born from people who can't accept the fact they're dead."

My eyes began to adjust to the dim light— where was it coming from? I twisted and turned, hoping to spy a way out.

A bunch of strange screens, or mirrors—I couldn't tell which—hung from the walls. I saw a few tables lined up around the room with dusty beakers, test tubes, and rubber tubes perched on top of them, things you'd expect to find in a science lab.

"We aren't dead," I repeated and gave Bo a pinch on the arm for good measure. Inhaling deep, I noted how easily my lungs

B.K. Crawford

expanded and thanked God for an ample supply of oxygen.

"Maybe it takes time," Bo suggested, his teeth rattling with anxiety, "Maybe we're so far down, it'll take Granddaddy a few minutes to find us."

I took in another breath of gratitude as I realized I still had my field bag strapped to my shoulder. We had water, a few pieces of candy, and a flashlight—scant supplies. We needed to find a way out. I dug into the bag to withdraw the flashlight. Turning it on, I shined it in Bo's face.

"We aren't dead yet. But if we don't find a way out of here, that could change. Are you with me?"

He nodded, but I could see his fright and confusion remained.

"I have to pee," he said, bashfully.

"Ghosts don't pee. See? You're not dead."

He let out a long breath of air, finally convinced. I told him to go find a dark corner to relieve himself. I did all my peeing on the way down.

I quickly surmised from our surroundings that we weren't the first to visit this place. Obviously, someone else had been here to build this room and set up the equipment. I felt a bit relieved at that because it meant someone else had come and gone, accessing the shaft freely. A way out existed, we just had to find it.

While Bo tended to his bladder, I inspected the room. The walls were smooth, much like the floor; a glossy, glass-like tempered metal. The reflection of my flashlight bounced off of it like a mirror. I searched for light switches, but didn't find any. I found no wires connected to the screens hanging on the walls either. I focused on the walls, searching for seams that might indicate a doorway, but couldn't locate anything of the sort. A panel on the east wall housed buttons and levers, gauges and dials. Not knowing what might happen if I touched them, I left them alone, curious if one of the controls might activate a secret door. If all else failed, I would come back to the panel as a last resort.

Bo gasped like someone who awoke to find a large, scary spider sprawled over his face. I swung the flashlight toward the sound. He stood beside one of the tables, frozen, pointing at the surface. I slowly walked toward him, fearful of what I might

B.K. Crawford

find. When I saw the objects on the table, I realized I would have been more satisfied with a wriggling arachnid, even an especially large one, especially hairy, and with sharp fangs.

Skeletons.

Human skeletons.

Sort of. They looked human. Kinda.

The largest of the skeletons stretched out over fourteen feet. The smallest, only six inches. All-in-all, we counted seven skeletons arrayed on the table, their skulls misshapen, the eye sockets different sizes and shapes. I gasped and took Bo by the arm, jerking him away from the morbid display.

"Where are we?" He panted. "Oh my God, we're in Hell. I told you we were dead."

I couldn't say where we were—I had no idea—but I wouldn't have guessed Hell. For one thing, hell isn't supposed to be cold.

"Did you pee?" I asked.

"Oh, yeah. Ghosts don't pee."

"Definitely not." I rubbed his shoulder, hoping to relieve some of the tension, then I took him by the hand. "Come on, there has to be a way out. Let's find it."

Bo clung to me like we were sewn together at the hip. I didn't blame him one

B.K. Crawford

bit; I had the flashlight. I told him not to touch anything weird and explained we were looking for a seam in the walls. We went over and over the walls and couldn't have inspected them any better if we'd used a microscope, but there wasn't a single ripple in the metal. Still, we searched, again and again, convinced we'd somehow missed a door.

"You might as well kiss me, because we're gonna die," Bo declared after an hour of searching. "There's no door, those flashlight batteries won't last forever and we're bound to run out of water. We're stuck in one of Jules Verne's spaceships. That's what this is. There's no way out."

Poor Bo. I understood his panic, but my thoughts kept returning to the panel on the east wall. Maybe it had a switch to activate an escape route. Then again, maybe pushing one of those buttons would bring the whole place crashing down on our heads. How could we know?

"What did you say?"

"I said you might as well kiss me."

"No. About Jules Verne."

"I said it's like we're stuck in one of his spaceships."

B.K. Crawford

"What makes you think so?"

He scratched his head. "Look at all this weird stuff. Skinny screens with no wires, dusty science experiments, screwy symbols, and the...*remains*. It's freaky."

"Symbols? What symbols?"

"Over in the corner, where I went pee."

"Show me."

Bo took me by the hand and we snaked around the tables. As we passed by, I noted some interesting objects I'd like to inspect after Bo showed me the symbols. He guided me to the west end of the room where someone erected an eight-foot obelisk. I shined the flashlight over its surface.

"They're Egyptian hieroglyphs," I muttered, shining the light from top to bottom.

"Can you read them?"

I ran my fingertips over the ancient engravings. "No. Just bits and pieces. This symbol means water and that one is the sun. I don't know enough to decipher any of it. I hoped to pick up a few classes in college."

"There's another stone, over here," Bo tugged on my arm. "Don't step in the puddle." He turned me toward a large statue behind the obelisk.

B.K. Crawford

Bright and colorful, the statue depicted the pointy black canine head of Anubis, his arms stretched out to his sides, as he looked to an opening far above his head. The artist had etched three successive pyramidal symbols beneath his feet.

"It's Anubis," I said, and Bo crinkled his brow.

"He's the jackal-headed god of the underworld. He decides which souls are allowed to enter the world of the dead."

Worry returned to Bo's face. "I told you we were dead."

"We aren't dead. Anubis isn't exactly the type you'd want to invite to your next birthday party, but it isn't at all odd to find him on Egyptian hieroglyphs. It would be odd if you didn't. It doesn't mean anything."

My words soothed Bo, but only slightly.

Ever since Daddy found the crystal ankh, the same question clawed at the back of my mind: Why did we find Egyptian artifacts buried on the North American continent, a world away from any place you'd commonly find such things? The ankh, the beetle, the lizard, an obelisk, and a stela. All distinctly Egyptian. It seemed like adding two plus two and getting seven instead of four.

B.K. Crawford

I spent twenty minutes looking over the hieroglyphs but didn't know any more than when I'd begun. Defeated, I suggested we take a look at some of the objects on the tables.

We found a pair of dusty goggles, unlike any I'd seen before. The viewing portion of the visor went ear-to- ear without a nosepiece for separation, as you would expect from a normal pair of glasses. I wiped the dust from the surface to find a dark film lurking beneath.

"Sunglasses?" Bo asked.

"A protective lens of some sort," I agreed. "Maybe they're used to shield the eyes from lab chemicals."

Bo nodded. "No sun down here," he sighed.

I looked over the head strap, but didn't find any adjustment loops. "One size fits all," I said, slipping the goggles over my head.

I wish I hadn't.

It felt like someone locked my head in a vice as the goggles gripped me. Pinpricks jabbed into my temples and my struggle to remove the offending apparatus proved in vain. Panicked, Bo tried to help, but only

B.K. Crawford

made things worse. The harder we pulled the more the goggles squeezed.

"Stop, stop, *stop*." I screeched, frantic to rid myself of the increasing pressure. Oddly, the pressure lessened when I stopped struggling. I took several deep breaths, trying to calm myself. Something inside the goggles activated and I began to see shimmering lights.

"I see something," I reported, reaching out for Bo's hands.

"A pink lotus flower. It's blooming. It looks so real, like I could reach out and touch it."

"A flower?"

"Yeah, it's like a movie. Wait. It's gone dark again. Wait. Whoa. There are millions of white dots, zooming by really fast. Whoa. Dizzy. There's this blue milky stuff. And now, bright light again."

My head twisted and turned as the views switched, and I began to feel nauseous as the pictures changed too fast.

"Patterns. Circles inside circles. Different shapes multiplied over and over. Lots of colors. Wow."

B.K. Crawford

My muscles jerked when the images I saw started to explode and a series of brilliant colors filled me with a sense of awe.

The next thing I knew, my eyes ached under the flashlight beam Bo had concentrated on my face. He stood over me with a canteen in his hand, my face soaked in water.

"You fainted," he explained and helped me to my feet.

"How'd you get the goggles off?" I asked.

"They fell off when you fainted. I thought the glasses melted your brain. It was awful."

I wrapped my arms around his waist and hugged him. He earned it.

After grappling with the goggles, I decided we wouldn't mess with any more of the objects on the tables. Lord knows what else might happen. From here on, we would focus on getting out.

I went back to the panel on the east wall and studied every button, dial, and lever. Despite not being able to find a door, I remained convinced there had to be an escape route somewhere. At the same time, I felt leery about touching the panel, especially after the incident with the goggles. It didn't cost anything to look, though.

B.K. Crawford

Most of the controls on the panel were marked by color; the operator would have had to memorize the different shades to know their function. Without a graph or a manual, I only saw a jumbled mess, a guessing game. Except for one large silver lever. Beneath it I found a raised symbol. The same symbol I'd seen on the Anubis stela.

Bo and I went back to the stela to study it again.

Anubis. Arms stretched wide. Looking up. The pyramidal symbols under foot.

I stared for a minute, thinking.

"What's it mean?" Bo asked, impatient.

I remembered the invisible hands that reached out to catch us on our way down and the hissing. I looked closer at the symbols beneath Anubis's feet—triangles with lines intersecting the top third of each. Were these air symbols? Anubis looked to a light far above his head with three of these symbols nestled beneath his feet. Had someone left a map of sorts, showing us the way out?

"I'm not sure, but I think it means we're going home for dinner."

"Really?"

B.K. Crawford

I nodded. "Like I said, I'm not sure." I
leaned in for a closer look at the area over
Anubis's head. "It's worth a shot."

We returned to the center of the room.

"We need to look at this floor," I said,
taking the whisk brush out of my field bag.
"Look close. See if you can find a seam."

I brushed dust and debris away. In a few
minutes I had located a seam. About six feet
in circumference, the seam formed a wide
circle.

"Stand here," I told Bo, directing him to
the center of the circle.

"Why?" He blurted, nervous.

"Because you're going home."

"Alone?"

"I'm not sure. Maybe. I'll try to get back
to the circle in time to go with you, but I
don't know how this works. You might have
to go alone and wait for me."

He shook his head, objecting.

"There's no other way," I insisted. "Well,
maybe there is, but we can't find it. Just
stand there and don't move."

"You're a bossy woman, Jennifer Jane
Houston."

I made my way back to the panel and
gripped the lever.

B.K. Crawford

"If I don't make it back, go get help."

I pulled the lever.

The hissing began once the lever dropped all the way down and its intensity increased quickly. I rushed back toward the circle. Bo had already begun to hover, his feet a foot off the ground.

"*Run*," He yelled.

Diving for the center of the circle, I crashed into Bo's ankles just as the pressure built beneath us and lifted us back up into the hole.

Except for the darkness, our ascent went smoothly and comfortably, although, going up took a lot longer than coming down.

"How'd you know that would work?" Bo asked.

"I didn't. I just guessed."

"So, for all you knew, when you pulled the lever, a giant scorpion could've burst through the floor and eaten us both?"

"I suppose. But there were no scorpions in the picture with Anubis. Sometimes, you gotta go with your gut."

We returned to the crystal cave and the gate closed behind us. I warned Bo to stay away from the stalagmite that had opened the gaping hole.

B.K. Crawford

We gathered our things. Fortunately, Daddy's lamp was intact, but we'd been underground for so long, it ran out of fuel. I swore Bo to total secrecy. He wasn't to breathe a word to anyone. I would decide later whether or not to tell Daddy.

Bo assured me he was okay to go home alone, so we agreed to go our separate ways when we got back to Moon Street. Before he left, I reminded him he'd promised to go see Phoebe Hornbrook with me.

"That was *before* we almost died in hell," he moaned.

"You're not going back on your word?"

He actually thought about it. He stood there with his hands shoved in his pockets and *thought* about it.

Dropping his chin to his chest, he kicked a stone. "You're a dangerous woman, J.J."

I felt my cheeks burn. "It wasn't my idea to go to the dig site. You begged, practically got on your knees. So, don't give me lip about who's dangerous. If you want to back out on your promise, just say so, but don't blame it on me."

He took his ball cap off and dragged his fingers through muddy hair.

B.K. Crawford

"I never said I'd go back on my word. I'll go with you to see the crazy lady. I just said you're dangerous is all. It's been a long day. I'm tired, I'm hungry, I'm beat."

Maybe I'd misread him.

"I'm sorry. I thought you were backing out. I guess I'd understand if you did. It just feels easier when you're around. Maybe I'm tired, too."

He gave me a pat on the shoulder and told me to come to the farm when I wanted to go see Phoebe.

And they say women are hard to read.

B.K. Crawford

A Whole Nest Of Evil

ВЖВ

The weather couldn't have been more perfect for a walk on Bear Claw mountain.

I met Bo at the farm in the morning, helped him finish his chores and apologized again for not trusting him to keep his word. Like it was my fault.

I'd packed his favorite for lunch, a big slab of bologna and half a pound of sharp cheddar. I threw a couple bananas in for good measure, along with a quart of strawberry ale.

The walk relaxed us as we climbed the hillside road, the sun beating on our shoulders, a world away from yesterday's horrors. It felt good to joke and laugh again, it felt good to be alive.

We found Phoebe Hornbrook weaving an elaborate tapestry on her porch, her silver hair tied back in a long braid. She seemed in a daze as she gazed off, seeing Lord knows what, while her fingers worked tapestry threads from memory. It amazed me to realize she had perfected her craft so masterfully she could probably weave in her sleep if she wanted. I hoped maybe,

B.K. Crawford

someday, I might master something half as well.

Phoebe's hands went still and she sat up straight, looking for the source of the twig snapping that alerted her to our presence. We strode through the tree line and approached apprehensively.

Her gray eyes locked on me as we came forward.

"You again?" She snickered, like she couldn't believe I had the nerve to come back after what she'd said about cooking children.

Summoning my courage, I pointed at Bo and said, "We were wondering if you might answer a few questions about your brother, Hank."

Her already wrinkled nose scrunched up in disgust. "You ain't mixed up with that sidewinder, are ya?" She raised her chin and shook her head. "There's a man who never had a marble to spare."

"You mean he's nuts?" Bo prodded.

Her eyebrows raised and the slightest hint of a twitch played at the corners of her mouth.

"He fits in, when he wants. But don't be fooled. Made my life miserable when we were kids. Was a mighty fine day when he

B.K. Crawford

finally went off to school and left for good. I was relieved for it, and so were the cats."

"The cats?" Bo asked, getting comfortable on a porch step at Phoebe's feet. The boy had nerve. She looked at him the way someone would look at an offensive bug, unsure if she wanted to stomp him or not.

"He used to throw kittens into the barn fan, just to watch 'em splat."

I gasped and recoiled at the thought.

"No he didn't," Bo said, disgusted.

Phoebe nodded. "Never owned up to it, denied it every time, but I saw him do it more than once. Never seen a young boy take more pleasure. It tickled him to the bone."

Wide-eyed, Bo and I stared at each other.

"I had some pity for him," she continued, "because of the way our Momma used to parade him around in his little cowboy outfits, but I lost all care when he started to take his frustration out on me." Her face drooped and her gaze went blank, the way a body does when difficult memories come to call.

"Cowboy outfits?" I squeaked, my nerves not quite over the cat story.

She snapped out of her trance, eyes blinking a wild flutter. "Our daddy was a

B.K. Crawford

rancher from Wyoming. Died just before
Hank was born. I expect dressing Hank up
like a cowboy soothed Momma's grieving
soul, but Hank hated it. Caused a lot of hissy
fits and crying, but Momma always got her
way."

   Bo and I locked gazes again.

   "Miss Hornbrook," Bo stuttered, "Do you
think your brother could be a murderer?"

   Her jaw clenched, her lips went thin and
her eyes shifted between the two of us. "I'd
say it's likely the good Lord forgot to give him
a soul."

   I fumbled through my field bag until I
found the threatening letter I'd received.
Offering it to her, I asked if she thought it
looked like something her brother would do.
She glanced at the envelope, took the letter
out, read it, bobbed a sharp nod, and pointed
at the face of the envelope.

   "The stamp is a special issue used by state
officials," she said. "Lord, you can't trust
government to begin with and when they
hire men like Hank you have to figure there's
a whole nest just like him. All the more
reason to keep your distance and mind your
own business. That's what I do. I suggest
you do the same." She handed me the letter,

B.K. Crawford

stood to her feet, and walked into her house, closing the door without another word.

"She's not very neighborly," Bo observed as we pushed through the trees and made our way back to the road.

"We did show up uninvited," I countered. "And the topic of conversation wasn't exactly pleasant. I don't imagine I'd feel neighborly if someone came poking into my past without a warning. I'd say we're lucky she talked to us at all."

"I guess you're right," Bo grunted. "She sure gave us plenty to think about."

That, she had. Bo and I chattered on about it the whole way home. It seemed obvious Hank Hornbrook had killed those young boys, stuffed them into cowboy outfits, and hung them up in the basement. Revenge of a sick sort for what his Momma did to him. As much as I tried, I just couldn't accept the fact that people who had it in them to do such a thing could exist on the same planet with people like me and Bo. I wondered why it had to be that way. Some questions, though, feel too big for answers. And, questions like that, I suspect, will turn a body into a rabid dog chasing its own tail. It's maddening if the dog never catches his tail

B.K. Crawford

and a painful thing when he does. So, I dropped it like a hot rock and focused on what we'd learned from the witch of Bear Claw mountain.

It seemed fairly certain Hank Hornbrook had mailed the threatening letter to me. We were also convinced Hank was the one who beaned Bo at the carnival. Hank worked with Mr. Newhouse, whose son I'd discovered hanging in the basement. And now we knew for a fact Hank's veins ran with venom. But, we still had no proof. And the reason we had no proof wasn't so much a fault on our part, but because someone had moved Davey Newhouse's body from the Hornbrook basement. How did Hank Hornbrook know to get the body out with only minutes to spare?

Something Phoebe said about the government flashed in my head like a neon sign. *'A whole nest just like him.'*

Of course. Hank wasn't in this alone. Someone at the police force might've tipped him off when Daddy called them. A spy. I'd put my money on Lieutenant Shafer. Maybe she brought that photo of Davey by just to see how much I knew about the case. Maybe she kept her mouth shut about seeing me at

B.K. Crawford

the church just to keep Daddy in the dark.
But, why would the police cover for a killer?
And, if they were protecting a criminal, what
good would it do to call them for help?

B.K. Crawford

Miss Tilly On A Cliff

ВЖВ

Bo and I blabbed until our constant chatter gave me an idea. We'd made good time going up the mountain, our talk with Phoebe didn't last long, and we were back on Moon Street before noon. We still had time to do some more investigating if I could convince Miss Tilly to cooperate with my plan. I told Bo what I had in mind and asked if he wanted to come along. He said he couldn't go because he had chores, which is just his way of getting me to offer to help. I promised to pitch in with the hog slopping when we got back, so off we went to visit Miss Tilly.

We caught her on a quiet day. Seems a fox went after Mr. Warble inside the outhouse and when the chicken disappeared into one of the dump holes, the fox attacked Pappy, probably out of frustration. So, Miss Tilly needed to make some sewing repairs; she had thread hanging from her mouth when we walked in the door.

"Miss J.J.," she squealed with delight. "And Mr. Bo. What a pleasant surprise."

B.K. Crawford

She put her sewing down and clapped her hands to her cheeks with excitement. "We'll have tea and crumpets. I'll find something nice for us to wear and we'll have a séance. See if we can drum up Jack Benny. Won't that be fun?"

I cut her off at the pass. "No. It's not dark enough for a séance and Jack Benny isn't dead."

"He isn't?"

"No. Besides, we have a better idea. Don't we, Bo?"

Bo stammered and gave me a cranky look for putting him on the spot. "Yeah," he said, playing along, "We sure do."

"Wouldn't it be fun," I coaxed, "if we had a parade for the queen?"

Miss Tilly's eyes lit up and her smile spread wide. She took the bait, I just had to reel her in.

"You could get dressed up and take your car out of the barn. We'll drive to town and wave to the queen the whole way."

Lord, she looked like she might burst with joy.

"Really? You would do that?"

We nodded with enthusiasm, goofy grins pasted on our faces.

B.K. Crawford

J. J. HOUSTON ©194
Murder on Moon Street

She clapped her hands with glee.

"Wait right there," she tittered, heading for her chest of moth-ridden treasures.

When she came back, she wore a brown fur stole over her shoulders and a jeweled tiara with see-through lace attached to it. The lace covered her face and fell to her bosom. White gloves, studded purse, mint green skirt, mint green jacket and purple pumps. If not for the shoes, she'd look like Betty Davis incognito.

Reaching to a shelf over the sink, she grabbed an old tin box and wrestled with it until the top popped off. Pulling out a set of keys, she handed them to Bo.

"If you wouldn't mind bringing the car around, kind sir," she said, batting her eyelashes.

Five minutes later, Bo leaned on the horn of Miss Tilly's white and blue 1959 Dodge Coronet to let us know we were ready to go. I took Miss Tilly by the elbow and guided her out the door. She shooed Bo out of the driver's seat, so he hopped into the backseat with me.

Miss Tilly took the wheel.

B.K. Crawford

I gave my best argument as to why we should take the safe roads to town, but Miss Tilly wouldn't hear a word of it, insisting, instead, on taking the scenic route.

See, there's a stretch of highway leading into town with about a mile of cliff road. It's so high up, if you're brave enough to stand by the side of the road and look down, you won't see to the bottom. The only thing to stop a driver from flying into the arms of the abyss is a mangled aluminum guard rail. The thing is, Miss Tilly never really learned how to drive properly, but uses the car's hood ornament like a divining rod. She doesn't watch her mirrors, or the road, because all her focus is devoted to making sure the ornament is aimed at the center line. This unfortunate practice is a thorn in Daddy's side and the subject of more than one argument between him and Momma; battles he wins when he insists only a suicidal idiot gets in a car with Miss Tilly behind the wheel.

Yes, I knew this. But, one: I did try to talk her into taking another route. And, two: I had no other choice if I wanted to get to town. So, I held my breath and my tongue, praying God would clear the cliff of all other traffic because, soon, Miss Tilly's Dodge

B.K. Crawford

would hog the center line on a thin road normally populated by monstrous freight trucks in a hurry to get to their destinations.

We were still rattling over Moon Street when Miss Tilly reminded us to wave to the queen, so we rolled down the windows and paid homage to the old goat. Some folks, out working their gardens, or taking a stroll, humored us and waved back. Now and again, a dog would jump onto the road to chase the car but each of them gave up with a snarl and a shrug when they realized we were too easy to catch.

"It's okay to go a little faster," Bo prodded.

Miss Tilly flicked a gloved wrist at him. "The car gets dirty when the dust kicks up."

Bo shook his head.

I knew she drove slow because there ain't no lines on a dirt road. That made her hood ornament useless and she was scared silly to drive without it.

To be fair, most folks do drive cautiously down Moon Street because it's full of ruts, but it is safe to do more than the five miles an hour Miss Tilly almost achieved.

"She'll speed up once we get to the hard road," I assured Bo, knowing Miss Tilly never drives faster than thirty-five miles an hour.

B.K. Crawford

Given her dangerous driving technique, we could at least thank the good Lord she didn't have a lead foot.

She reminded us, several times, to keep waving. I still had some groundwork to accomplish, so once we took to the paved roads and Miss Tilly had accelerated all the way up to twenty-five, I leaned forward until my lips were behind her ear and said, "The salon has a special running all week. Half off. I read it in the paper."

"Oh!" She squealed with delight. "How much is half?"

"Paper said two dollars for shampoo, cut, curl, and dye."

"Grab my purse, Honey, see if there's two dollars in there. Oh, I wish I'd known before we left home."

I reached over the seat, snagged the purse and rifled through it until I found her money bag. Fourteen dollars and seventeen cents. I told her she had plenty to spend and this excited her so much, she stepped on the gas. At last we were zooming along at thirty miles an hour.

"Oh, but it takes a couple hours at the salon. I wouldn't want to make you wait," she moaned.

B.K. Crawford

"That's okay," I patted her on the shoulder. "The salon is only a block from the library. We'll wait there and you can pick us up when you're finished."

"Are you sure you won't mind?" She turned all the way around to inspect our expressions and drove straight into a ditch.

Once our screeching and shrieking died down, Bo got out of the car to survey the damage. Mud on the flap and a few dings in the hubcap. It could have been a whole lot worse.

"All you have to do is back up and you're out," he told her. "But, listen, I can drive. I know I'm young and I ain't got a license, but I've been driving on the farm for a couple years and I do right well. I'd be happy to get us to town. Please let me drive, Ma'am."

Miss Tilly thanked Bo for his sweet offer, but wouldn't hear of it. After that, she did slow down to twenty miles an hour and kept a keen focus on the hood ornament.

As we approached the cliff road, Miss Tilly continued to aim for the center line. Bo's eyes went wide and he suggested she move to the right some. Didn't do any good. She only knew the one way to drive. We prayed every inch of the way and clung white-

B.K. Crawford

knuckled to the door handles. On two separate occasions, freight trucks came barreling toward us, both pushing the fifty-five mile an hour speed limit. The truckers laid on their horns, but Miss Tilly held her ground, forcing them to drive on the berm of the road, inches from the guard rails and two feet from oblivion. The car rocked from the wind pressure as the eighteen wheelers blew by.

I decided right then—even if it cost me college, my first born, and a lifetime supply of crumpets and tea—I would find a way to convince her to go home the other way. My nerves would surely not survive another ten minutes of Miss Tilly on a cliff.

When we finally pulled into the parking lot in front of the hair salon, Miss Tilly said she'd come to the library once she finished with her primping. Bo and me got out of the car, but stood panting on the sidewalk until the blood circulation returned to our legs again. Then we made our way to the library.

Founded in 1897, the public library resembles a miniature castle. Most of the buildings in town are very old and harbor a historic feel, but none so much as the library. Only a blind man could miss the majesty of

B.K. Crawford

the red brick building roosting high on its hill.
We walked the long sidewalk and climbed
the cement stairs that lead to an archway
that housed the front door. The perfect
gentleman, Bo opened the door and ushered
me inside. With only a couple hours to
accomplish our mission, I went straight to the
front desk.

"Hello," I said to the pretty woman sitting
behind the counter. She put down the book
she'd been reading and gave us a beaming
smile.

"How can I help you?"

"Do you have a record of the local
obituaries?"

She nodded. "How far back?"

I didn't quite know how to answer and
kicked myself for not being better prepared.

"Two years," I said, but my answer sounded
more like a question than a statement.

"Lou is in charge of those." She reached
for the phone. "He's a statistics nut, loves
that sort of thing." She dialed and when
someone picked up the other end, she said,
"Lou? We have some youngsters here who
would like to see two years on the obits.
Mmmhmm. Okay, thank you."

B.K. Crawford

She put the phone back on its cradle and pointed to a hallway on her left. "Second door on the right. You can go on in."

The hallway felt dark and creepy, but I suppose my nerves were still doing the jitterbug from the drive into town. We found the door and Bo knocked. A voice from the other side called to us, "Come in. It's open."

A tall, fit fellow sitting behind a big desk stood to his feet, reached to offer us each a hand shake, and introduced himself. "I'm Lou." He motioned for us to take a seat at a long conference table. "Miss Fontain tells me you're looking for obits. Two years, right?"

Bo nodded, but I asked for more. "Do you have five years?"

Lou grinned. "Little lady, I can take you back a hundred years if you have the time."

"We don't."

He chuckled.

"Five years then. That takes us back to 1958," he murmured, ruffling through a stack of oversized ledgers on his desk. He selected three ledgers and brought them to us.

"That should keep you busy. I'm on my way out for a late lunch. If you have any

B.K. Crawford

questions, ask Miss Fontain at the front desk. You'll find she's very helpful."

Lou grabbed his suit jacket off the back of his chair and left us to explore.

I opened the cover of the first ledger. January, 1958. Closing that, I reached for the ledger on the bottom.

"We'll start with last year and work our way back," I said. "That way, if we run out of time, we might still have something to go on. Grab a pencil and paper."

Bo took a pencil out of a cup at the center of the table, along with a legal pad and sat back down, leaning in for a look at the ledger.

Scanning the pages, I skipped over the majority of the entries because they belonged mostly to old folks.

"Here's one. Write this down. February 22, 1962, Steven Ollivander, nine years old, passed away unexpectedly. No photograph."

While Bo scratched the information onto the tablet, I resumed the search.

"March 22, 1962, Andrew Scott, ten years old, passed away unexpectedly. No photograph. March 28, 1962, Emily Vandstant, nine years old, drowned. There's a photo. Poor kid."

B.K. Crawford

"I remember that one," Bo said, "still writing on the pad, "Fell through the ice on a pond near her place. My Dad knows the family."

"That has to be hard. I can't even imagine."

"Me either," Bo said.

"How do you even get out of bed after something like that?"

"I don't know. But, tick, tick, tick. Time's a wasting."

"Hmm? Yeah, you're right." I resumed the search.

"June 23, 1962, Todd Beck, twelve years old, passed away unexpectedly. No photograph. June 15, 1962, Denise Ford, ten years old, passed after a battle with leukemia. She has a photograph."

As time passed, we toured the ledgers and discovered an emerging pattern. When I first thought about coming to the library, I had a wild hunch, one I hoped wouldn't come to anything, but by the time we finished compiling our list, Bo had also picked up on the pattern.

Based on what we found, it looked as though someone had killed a local boy once a month, every month—on or around the last week of the month—for the past five years. The paper listed these fatalities as 'passed away unexpectedly,' and never attached a photograph to the obituary. As if we didn't find that frightening enough, we realized these deaths were only for our county. When I mentioned this to Bo, he went to Lou's desk and found a ledger for an adjacent county, also listing obituaries for 1962. Dreadfully, we found the same pattern there, and in several other counties as well.

There are sixty-seven counties in the state.

On another hunch, based on what Phoebe Hornbrook said about a nest of evil, we did some more cross-referencing only to find many of the victims on our list were related in some way to public officials. Council members, aides, judges, all the way up to the congress and the senate. Seeing this, Bo slammed his fist on the table. "That's it, J.J., you're in over your head."

Lord, I knew he was right.

B.K. Crawford

An Accidental Murderer

ВЖВ

A few more hours at the library surely would have given us a lot more to go on, but time went by like a bob-tailed nag training for the Camptown racetrack.

Miss Tilly came back from the salon with hair to match her shoes—a mortifying shade of purple. She seemed so pleased with her hair, she didn't argue when I insisted on taking the safe route home. We made it back to Moon Street in time to do Bo's evening chores.

After I'd tossed the last pail of slop, I went home with our research notes stuffed securely in my pocket. There, I helped Momma scrub the dinner dishes and went to my room, exhausted. The day had practically flown by and I could barely believe the clock had struck six-thirty already. The sun would shine for another few hours and I could hear Daddy gouging weeds from the garden with his spade. Normally, I'd give him a hand, but I felt like a comatose rock. So, I kicked off my sneakers without untying them and plopped on the bed, ready to read through the notes Bo wrote at the library.

B.K. Crawford

It would have taken days, maybe weeks, to record all the names of the victims whose obituaries fit our criteria, but we did manage to gather a large list.

Unlike most kids our age, Bo has neat handwriting, pleasant and easy to read, even though he'd scribbled the list in a rush. I wondered if he got good grades in school. Then I wondered why I wondered.

There are four windows in my bedroom, so it gets tons of light and, along with the light, too much heat in the summer. I got back up to plug in an old fan Daddy picked up at the local scrap yard and immediately felt grateful for it despite the way it grumbled and moaned. Resuming my position on the bed, I went back to the list, feeling I might have missed something important in the rush at the library.

While I read, I wondered what reason people might have for covering up the deaths of their own children. It seemed obvious the parents were involved, or had at least been forced to keep quiet while their children went missing—lying to everyone around them, like Davey Newhouse's parents lied to Alice. What a dreadful secret to keep.

B.K. Crawford

I read through the list. Five pages in, I found an entry that froze the blood in my veins. Bolting to a sitting position, I clocked my head on the frame of the upper bunk. Rubbing the sore spot, I stared at the name, reading it over and over and over again, hoping it would change if I focused hard enough. It didn't.

How I'd missed this at the library, I couldn't say. Maybe I'd read the obituaries too fast and didn't really pay attention after the first dozen or so. Maybe I just didn't put two and two together. But I did now.

If there's such a thing as an accidental murderer, surely I fit the description. I began to feel dizzy and nauseous. Had banging my head caused the room to spin? Or, did the realization I'd just made turn the wrenches in my stomach? Either way, I rushed to the bathroom and threw cold water over my face. The reflection of an idiot quivered inside the mirror.

Still not willing to believe what I'd read, I rushed back to the list and read the entry one more time: *August 25, 1960, Virgil Flint, eleven years old, passed away unexpectedly. No photograph.*

B.K. Crawford

I'd sent Joey off to the Mountains with the Flints. Could this family possibly be involved with a nest of murderers? People who targeted boys his age? I doubted it. In my experience, they were gentle, caring people. But, if anything happened to Joey, the blame would lay forever in my pocket. I would never forgive myself.

I rifled through the mail on top of my dresser, pulling out the postcards I'd received from Joey, looking at the dates. The last one came in five days ago. Barefoot, I thumped down the stairs and rushed to the table where Momma keeps the mail. Flipping through the envelopes, I prayed for another post card. Nothing. Maybe no one collected the mail. I ran outside. Momma yelled at me for letting the screen door slam, but I was halfway to the mailbox by then.

Between the advertisements and a bill from the electric company, I found a post card. I pulled it away from the rest of the mail. Postmarked two days ago, it had a pretty picture of the sun setting over a lake. On the back, Joey had written three words. 'You're dead, J.J.'

Maybe, I thought, *but so are you and all because of me.*

B.K. Crawford

I carried the mail into the house and wiped a stream of tears from my eyes as I went back to my room. The Flints weren't scheduled to return for quite some time. That left plenty of opportunity for harm to come to Joey, if it hadn't already. I buried my face in my pillow, my body rocking as I cried. I couldn't possibly get in any deeper than this—I was slick to the hip, as the farmers like to say.

"What's all the fuss about?"

I lifted my face from my pillow and looked through blurry eyes to find Daddy standing there. I knew I had to tell him. What other choice did I have? Someone had to do something to try to save Joey. Daddy would beat me until my skin fell off in a pile at my feet, but I deserved it. I sat up, ready to tell him everything, but when I opened my mouth, a squeamish, "Nothing," squeaked out.

He snorted at that. "We raised two girls before you. Girls cry for a lot of reasons, but nothing is never one of them."

"I'm just missing Joey is all." I barely believed that lie came from my own mouth.

"Well, why don't you get out of bed and go call him?"

B.K. Crawford

"I can't call him, Daddy. I don't have the number for the campgrounds."

"He ain't in the mountains, kiddo. His Mom and Pop picked him up yesterday on their way back from Ohio and took him home. Now stop sniveling and go ring him up."

A wave of utter relief washed over me. Joey was safe. No harm had come to him after all. But, given how angry I'd made him, I really didn't want to give Joey an opportunity to rip into me over the phone.

"He's probably still mad at me. I'll call tomorrow, if that's okay."

"Fine," Daddy said and turned to leave. "Brush your teeth and get to bed."

I spattered toothpaste all over the mirror again. On the way back to my room, I dialed Aunt Celia's number. The phone rang four times, then Joey answered, so I hung up and went to bed.

B.K. Crawford

A Wrecked Heap
вжв

I like to draw and paint pictures. Daddy is the real artist in the family, though. When he draws and paints, he makes his pictures look so real you'd think you were looking at a photograph instead of a painting. Once, he did a portrait of Miss Tilly and left it on the dining room table to dry. While he was off taking care of other things, someone accidentally spilled a can of black paint on the canvas and ruined it. We never did find out who did it, but I suspected Dale because he made himself scarce for a week afterward.

After that, Daddy said he'd never paint again, at least not while he had kids still living at home. So, I borrowed his art instruction books and tried to learn how to draw from them. I don't know if I'll ever be as good as Daddy, but maybe if I keep taking baby steps, I might get there someday.

The reason I mention this is because one of the names on the list Bo and me took from the library belonged to my fourth grade art teacher, Mrs. Dunaway. A sweet woman. She always had a smile and a word of encouragement for every kid in her class.

B.K. Crawford

When she saw I had a genuine interest in learning to draw, she took to me like I was her own, saying I could be famous someday if I applied myself. I didn't think so, but I sure didn't mind trying. Now and then, Mrs. Dunaway would even invite me to her place on the weekends where we'd eat cookies and paint.

When I saw her name on the library list, I felt a heavy sadness settle on my heart and wondered if I hadn't seen her around school for the past two years because she'd lost her son. I'd bet on it.

I thought I should go see her. If I could talk to someone who lost a child in this mess, I might get some answers. But, then I thought it might be hard for her to talk about such a tragic loss. Torn, I didn't know which way to turn. In the end, I decided it worth the trouble if talking to Mrs. Dunaway could help save someone else's life. If she didn't want to talk about it, I'd just say hey and get on home.

And so, I packed a lunch and greased the chain on my bike.

The ride to Mrs. Dunaway's place took an hour and a half.

B.K. Crawford

A gray car with two flat tires sat in the driveway at the Dunaway house. I remembered the car from when Mrs. Dunaway used to buff the hood with a towel before she went to class. Now it looked like a wrecked heap.

I rode past a full mailbox. Letters and newspapers littered the ground, some of them fluttering against the wall of a shed twenty yards away. Several garbage cans choked on their contents as well and I wondered if the family had moved away. I'd come too far to leave without at least rapping on the door, so I dropped my bike on the overgrown lawn and approached the house.

I heard radio static coming from inside— the intermittent voice of a DJ broke through, then faded into garbled oblivion once again.

I found the main door open. Knuckles poised, I tapped on the screen door and stood there, waiting. And waiting. And waiting. I knocked again, but when no one answered, I peeked through a window.

I saw a dark form inside, rocking in a chair.

Heading back for the door, I knocked again. "Mrs. Dunaway, it's J.J. Houston. May I come in?"

B.K. Crawford

"Door's open," I heard her mumble, her tone drab.

Stepping over a pile of mail heaped on the floor, I entered the house and found her in the living room, rocking in her chair, a blank stare on her expressionless face. A bottle of alcohol dangled in her right hand, she hadn't washed her hair, and dark circles puffed like angry bruises under her eyes. Not at all the cheery woman I remembered.

She looked at me and failed to smile, her lips uncooperative. "I don't want to paint today," she slurred, her empty gaze moving away from me.

"I'm not here to paint. I came to ask about your son."

"Tommy?" She spurt, lifting her chin and turning to face me again.

I sat down in a stuffed chair beside her. "I'll understand if you don't want to talk about what happened."

"No," she murmured.

"You don't want to talk?"

She sighed with frustration and shook her head, "Just stay out of it. You'll get hurt."

"But there are others," I protested.

B.K. Crawford

"No one can do anything for them." She lifted her bottle and took a long swig, wiping her lips with her robe sleeve.

I didn't know what to say, so we sat in an awkward silence until she spoke again.

"They took his eyes. Chewed on his soul. They aren't human. They have no emotion. They're evil."

I gasped. "Who? Who are they?"

Tears streamed down her face and her hands began to tremble. She put the bottle of alcohol on the floor where it nearly tipped over. "They call themselves the gods," she whispered. "Heaven help us all."

I asked more questions, but she went comatose on me, sitting tight lipped and staring at the wall.

Doing what I could to comfort her, I gave her a hug and thanked her for talking to me. After I left, I blamed what she'd said on the alcohol and grief, but wondered if a sliver of truth might have been hidden somewhere in her statements.

On the way home I stopped at Miss Tilly's and told her about Mrs. Dunaway's condition. Miss Tilly went right to the phone, promising to get help.

B.K. Crawford

No one should have to suffer alone like that.

Old Magic
вжв

When I went to bed that night, Mrs.
Dunaway's desperate grief still weighed
heavily on my mind. By now, Miss Tilly had
found someone to care for her, but I said a
prayer anyway and skimmed through one of
my books, hoping to brighten my mood.

As I flipped through the pages of a thick
volume about the history of excavations in
Egypt, I remembered the beetle in my field
bag and recalled how strangely the crystals
acted when Daddy put them together. I
hadn't experimented with the beetle yet and
I wondered if it would glow like the lizard and
the ankh and, if so, what color it might have.

Tossing the book aside, I went to my closet
and opened the door. I found a violet hue
already radiating from the bag. Reaching in, I
carefully removed the beetle, instantly
enchanted with its beautiful glow. The
crystal felt warm in my hand and emitted the
sweetest lilac scent. I felt a strange sense of
giddiness as the stone's glow engulfed me, as
if I'd just heard the funniest joke ever. As
crystals go, I liked this one best. I basked in
the intoxicating scent of the crystal for quite

B.K. Crawford

some time before I thought again about the lizard and the ankh. Maybe if I put the crystals together, they'd do the same thing they did before.

The ankh glowed blue through the slats of my top dresser drawer and the lizard's green glow seeped out of a shoebox on the shelf. I put the beetle on the rug in the center of my room and snatched the other two pieces. Sitting on the floor, I placed each crystal so it faced the others in a makeshift triangle. This had an immediate effect as the glow from each piece melded with the color of the adjacent pieces, forming a pure white light. I heard a soft hum as the crystals began to vibrate. The vibration rate increased and a curious chirping made it seem as if the stones had something important to say to one another. The light became brighter still as the vibration increased. The crystals trembled, then lifted up and hovered a foot off the floor, spinning in a slow orbit. I quietly applauded, smiling in triumph. It happened exactly the way it did in the kitchen with Daddy.

Television has some pretty nifty magic shows, but none could hold a candle to this. I wished I could show my brothers and sisters

B.K. Crawford

what a magnificent find I'd discovered. And Miss Tilly, too. But, she would probably say what she always says, '*A miracle by any other name is magic*.'

Standing up, I looked down at the glowing crystals, slowly circling them, mesmerized by their graceful dance. Then a beam of light spread out like a peacock tail from the center of the stones and a shape began to take form within the arch.

"Hello," I heard a sweet voice say, and I turned toward the door, thinking someone had crept up behind me, but found no one there. When I turned back toward the stones, the face of a young girl had solidified inside the light. Smiling wide, she said, "My name is Karayah."

My heart began to pound like an animal caught inside a burning barn and fear overrode my senses. Despite the adrenaline rush, it took some doing to pry the crystals apart and get them back into their hiding places.

Panting on my bed, gulping for air, I wrapped my arms around myself and fought to calm my nerves. I must have fallen asleep and had a nightmare. That's what happened. I didn't really see a face at all, just a mirage, a

B.K. Crawford

wisp of a dream. Right? Yes. Of course.
Only a dream.

Daddy bellowed from behind my door,
"Go to sleep, J.J."

I said nothing, but thought, *I'm already
asleep, Daddy, and having a real bad dream.*

I gave it everything I had. I counted sheep,
I said the alphabet backwards, I hummed my
favorite tunes, I focused on my breathing, I
prayed, and I even thought about sneaking in
to sleep with Momma and Daddy, but
nothing worked.

Two hours after I put the crystals away, I
still saw the girl's face—still heard the sound
of her voice.   Try as I might, I couldn't
convince myself it was only a dream.

I thought about the pair of strange goggles
that threw me for a loop in the shaft at the
crystal cave. The unusual images the goggles
revealed seemed similar in some way to what
the crystals could do—eerie and frightening,
but tempting in an irresistible way. In fact, I
blame temptation for my decision to rescue
the goggles and bring them home. That's
right, I nabbed them, mostly because I
thought my brother, Danny, would get a kick
out of them. I couldn't find the backbone to
put them on again as the memory of the

B.K. Crawford

dizzying experience still remained fresh in my mind. So, I locked them up in a chest at the foot of the bunk beds where I intended to keep them until Danny came home.

The goggles and the glowing crystals came from the same cavern, which made me wonder if the crystal cave held some magical quality. Had a sorcerer, long, long, ago cursed the caves? That thought frightened me, so I didn't think it anymore. Instead, I focused on the Egyptians—a civilization known for developing strange technologies. Lord knows it isn't likely anyone will ever figure out how they built the pyramids with such exact precision, and Bo and me did find Egyptian hieroglyphs in the room at the end of the shaft. Maybe the goggles and the crystals were something the Egyptians invented. But, I still didn't understand how these artifacts ended up half a world away from the African continent.

I let my questions rest, knowing I wouldn't be able to sleep until I put the crystals back together to see what might happen next. The crystals were weird and frightening but, after a long quarrel with myself, I decided they hadn't really done anything dangerous. Not yet anyway.

B.K. Crawford

   Slipping out of bed, I went through the
routine exactly the way I did before and,
once again, the face of the same young girl
began to appear when the white light fanned
out into an arch. Ignoring the instinct to pry
the crystals apart again, I trembled so badly I
could barely stand as I stared at the face
forming in the shimmering light.

   "My friends call me Kara," the phantom
said, picking up where she left off.

   I leaked a little.

   Searching for courage, I heard Miss Tilly's
voice tittering in the back of my mind, *'Fear is
the result of too much assumption*.' So, I
decided to face only the facts. A recorded
film hooked up to a powerful projector could
cause the specter I saw before me. A movie,
only different...more present, more real.
Certainly, I had no reason to fear a silly
movie.

   This line of thinking offered me room to
breathe. But, as I slowly circled the image of
the miniature girl, her head twisted, as if she
could see me, her gaze following along as I
moved. Impossible. People in movies can't
actually see outside the screen. Can they?

   As if in answer, she complained, "You're
making me dizzy."

B.K. Crawford

Once again, I quelled an overwhelming desire to break the crystals apart. A barrage of questions formed in my mind so quickly, I could barely choose one.

"Who are... What are... Where are...," I whispered, failing to finish my thoughts.

"Stand still. Let me see you," she implored.

She seemed alive, not a recording at all. Stunned, I did as she asked.

"I am Karayah Shah, known to my friends as Kara. In my land, it's customary to exchange names. May I ask yours?"

Staring awkwardly, I answered, "J.J., Jennifer Jane Houston."

Curious, I reached out to touch her cheek, but my hand passed through her image, causing a ripple in the light.

"You're a *ghost.*"

"Not technically. I assume you found my crystals?"

Not a ghost. What then? A genie? Do I get three wishes? Or, was this something else altogether?

"Crystals? Oh, yes, yes, I found them," I stammered.

"Why are we whispering?"

"My parents are asleep."

B.K. Crawford

I tried to hide my fear, but my squeaky voice gave me away, "What are you?"

"Don't be afraid. I can't hurt you. It's a common practice among my people to preserve consciousness inside holograms as a method of passing knowledge from one generation to another. The crystals you found were part of my class project. Haven't you ever seen a hologram?"

I shook my head. "I don't even know what a hologram *is*. Is it like a telegram? We have telegrams, but most people don't use them anymore since we have telephones now." I could tell she didn't know what I meant from the quizzical expression on her face, so I explained.

"You pick up a receiver, dial a number, and if the person is home, they pick up their telephone and you can talk to each other. Even if you're half way around the world."

She seemed perplexed, but nodded.

"I don't think holograms are much like telephones. Holograms are exact duplicates of a person, place, or thing. They're three dimensional, as you can see. Much like a living letter. Only, I programmed mine so that only those on a similar vibration

B.K. Crawford

frequency can view it. I got an honorary mark in class for doing the extra work."

I scrunched my nose and scratched my cheek. "A similar...*what*?"

"Vibration." Seeing my confusion, she elaborated, "Like strings on musical instruments. If you tune two instruments together, you can get them to sound alike because the strings are vibrating on the same frequency."

"Oh." I was beginning to understand. "So, you and me, we vibrate the same?"

"Not exactly the same, but close enough to make our meeting possible."

She had a sweet smile.

"Can anyone make a hologram?"

"I believe there are many ways. I started by growing my crystals."

I found that interesting. "You can *grow* crystals?"

"Yes, easily. You can even shape them before they're seeded. I chose the ankh to represent soul or spirit, the lizard to represent the physical, and the beetle to represent the mind. Each of the crystals are programmed in different ways. For example, I programmed the lizard by allowing it contact with my skin for thirty days. I

B.K. Crawford

programmed the ankh with prayer and the beetle with direct focus. Once the crystals are charged, when they come into close proximity with one another, their light particles combine to create a complete representation of myself, such as you see now."

"This is a class project? Aren't you my age, like twelve?"

"Fourteen," she corrected me.

"The kids in my class are making batteries out of grapefruit juice," I nervously chuckled, embarrassed by what my teachers considered an adequate education.

Surely, with such advanced technology, this girl must come from the future. Or, did she? I wondered.

"When are you?" I asked.

"I don't understand."

"What year? What age, eon, era?"

"I live in the year 28000," she said.

Wow. 28000. My mind started reeling again.

"B.C. or A.D.?"

"I'm sorry, I don't recognize those distinctions."

"Can you tell me where you live? What it's like there?"

B.K. Crawford

"I live in the southern part of a beautiful paradise called Atland, by the sea. There are palm trees, tropical fruits, and plentiful grains when our growing fields are protected from the mastodon."

"Wait, did you say mastodon?"

"Yes, they are unruly beasts, impossible to tame, and very destructive."

Surprised, I cupped my face with the palms of my hands. The mastodon went extinct at the end of the Pleistocene age eleven thousand years ago.

"You're *B.C.*," I squealed, a little too loud for my own comfort. I hoped Daddy didn't hear.

"What is your era?" Kara asked.

"I'm 1963 A.D. About thirty thousand years after you."

We stared at each other in awe, a vast eternity looming between us. The trance broke when I heard Daddy's feet on the floorboards outside my door.

"I have to go," I screeched, breaking the crystals apart and shoving them into the field bag.

Daddy didn't say anything as he moved past my door on his way to the bathroom.

B.K. Crawford

If I found it difficult to sleep before, I didn't have a chance after talking to Kara. Part of me still didn't believe what I'd seen, while another part desperately wanted to know more.

I worried myself to sleep—what if Kara's crystals lost their charge, leaving me without a chance to talk to her again? What if I imagined it all? What if the stress and pressure of the insanities surrounding me this summer had cost me my last saltine? What if I ended up like Miss Tilly, half a cracker in a sea of loose soup?

B.K. Crawford

Lighting The Fire
ВЖВ

I awoke the next morning, trembling, after a horrible dream in which Mrs. Dunaway repeatedly cried, "They took my baby's eyes." Then I saw Hank wearing a bloody grin on his face, holding a limp infant in his arms.

Nightmares like that make me wish my brain came equipped with an eraser.

I felt worlds better after a warm bath and a bowl of hot oatmeal.

Momma and Daddy asked if I'd like to tag along on a grocery run and a trip to the post office. I said I promised to help Bo on the farm, so they waved goodbye as Daddy's truck kicked up a cloud of dirt.

I packed my things, greased the chain on my bike, and took off for the Duke farm.

When I arrived, I couldn't find Bo anywhere in sight, so I asked Mr. Duke where I might find him. He said the catfish were biting.

Abandoning my bike, I made my way through the high grass to the pond hidden behind the barn where I found Bo casting a line between the cattails. With his tackle box at foot, he stood next to a jiggling pail of

B.K. Crawford

frantic fish desperate to return to the muddy deep.

Hearing the sound of grass swooshing against my legs as I approached, Bo turned with a smile.

"Twenty-eight and a half inches," he said, excited and pointing at his pail.

"Nice one," I exclaimed, sidling up beside him.

"Still after the Granddaddy," he said, reeling in.

Bo and his father are forever competing to see who can reel in the, 'whopper of all whoppers.' Supposedly, the Granddaddy is over four feet long and ornery as a bull. In his determination to get the fish before his father, Bo had spent all of his money on tackle and a new pole.

"You sure he's even in there?"

"I've seen him jump," Bo declared, casting his line.

Bending over, I peeked under the lid of his pail to find close to a dozen slimy black fish fighting to get out.

"Jeez, how long you been out here?"

He laughed. "Only a couple hours. They seem especially stupid today."

B.K. Crawford

"Any chance I can steal you away? I've got something you need to see."

Groaning, he adjusted the brim of his ball cap. "You can't show me here?"

"Nope."

"Why not?" He fiddled with his line, reeling it in a turn or two.

"Well, for one, I don't want you getting mad at me if your fishing pole ends up in the pond."

"Why on God's green earth would that happen?"

"Trust me. You will never in your life see anything so strange or exciting."

He shifted his weight from one foot to the other and back again, sighing deeply.

"Bo, how long you been trying to catch that fish?"

He chuckled. "Since I was old enough to hold a pole."

"And, you really think today's the day?"

"Could be."

"All right. You stay and fish. I'm going to the barn. If you hear a loud explosion and the barn catches fire, just bring a bucket of water, okay?"

"What the..." He turned to complain, but I was already halfway across the field.

B.K. Crawford

"J.J. *wait*."

I laughed at the panic in his voice and the sound of his line reeling in.

Momma says there's only two ways to make a man put down a fishing pole—take away his beer, or light a fire under his ass. Bo's too young for beer, so fire seemed the only way to go.

Peeking over my shoulder, I saw him trip over himself in a rush to gather his things.

Bo's mood seemed sour when he finally joined me in the barn. I couldn't blame him for being mad, maybe he would've caught that fish if I hadn't come along. But, I felt like I might jump out of my skin for wanting him to meet Kara. Men catch fish every day. How many folks can say they've had a conversation with someone thirty thousand years old? So, while Bo might have a momentary thorn in his thumb, once he saw what I had to show him, he would understand why I dragged him away.

"What is it?" He seethed, glaring at me.

I tried to fight against my amusement, but a wry grin won the battle. The smirk only made Bo more angry.

"Come here." I moved him further into the barn, so as not to stand by the door where

B.K. Crawford

anybody could see what we were up to.
Taking my field bag off my shoulder, I opened
it. "Swear you'll never tell a soul."

"You don't ask for much," he said, his tone
flat.

"That fish will still be there in half an hour.
I rode all the way here just to show you
something amazing and all I get is attitude?"

He took a deep breath and softened his
expression.

I removed the crystals from the small
boxes I'd packed them in to keep them apart
and arranged them on the barn floor. I knew
right away I'd done something wrong
because the stones weren't glowing. In a
panic, I thought they'd lost their charge and
I'd dragged Bo away from his fishing for
nothing. Then I realized I'd never seen the
crystals glow in bright daylight. Maybe they
only work in a dark environment. Snatching
up the stones, I tugged on Bo's shirt and
dragged him to a shadowed corner in the
back of the barn.

Once I found a suitable spot, I set the
crystals up again. Bo gasped sharply as the
crystals began to glow. And again when they
vibrated. And again when their chirping
commenced. He about blew a gasket when

B.K. Crawford

they lifted off the floor and levitated. I held his hand tight, knowing his instincts would react like mine had when I first saw the spectacle.

"What is this?" He panted, his breathing erratic.

"Just watch. It's okay."

The colors melded and turned bright white as the stones began to orbit one another. Then the arch appeared and, inside it, Kara's face began to take shape.

Bo held his ground until he saw a face in the light, then he took me by the arms and tried to drag me away.

"*Get out*," He demanded.

The boy is strong on a normal day, but add a little adrenaline to the mix and he's a backwoods Hercules. I had to duck and tuck to get out of his grasp, willing my feet to stay planted.

"It's okay, she can't hurt you." To make my point, I reached out to pass my hand through the hologram so he could see Kara wasn't solid.

Wide-eyed, he stared as light particles scattered and rearranged themselves.

"She's like a pet ghost," I said and apologized to Kara for being so crude.

B.K. Crawford

Kara giggled, greeting us both with a cheery, "Hello."

Beaming, I looked at Bo only to find he'd gone ashen. Tearing the canteen out of my bag, I made him drink until he'd all but finished a quart of juice. Not wanting to put him through any more stress, I said good-bye to Kara, dismantled the crystals and put them away. I could always set them up again later.

Repeating the phrase like a broken record, Bo kept saying, "It's not safe."

I gave him time to catch his breath.

"She's perfectly safe. It's just a hologram. It can't hurt you."

"Not that. *You*. Keeping your company isn't safe. First you find a dead body, then you get threatening letters, then you hunt down the witch of Bear Claw mountain, then your killer hits me in the head. Now you've got ghosts trapped in stones. It's you, J.J. Being with *you* isn't safe."

He did have a point.

We sat in silence on a couple bales of hay for what seemed the longest time. Me, feeling badly for dragging him into all of this and he, overwhelmed with it, I guess. Bo finally broke the ice by asking, "What's a hologram?"

B.K. Crawford

I told him everything I knew about them.

"Is she from the future, another planet, or what?" He wanted to know.

"Actually, she's thirty thousand years old. After I talked to her last night, I looked up Atland in the encyclopedia. Atland is another name for Atlantis. Can you believe it?"

He shook his head. "It doesn't make sense. Her hologram is obviously advanced technology. You expect that from the future, not the past."

"You'd think so, based on what we've been taught. But archeologists uncover evidence of high technology on almost every major dig. They found the Baghdad battery dating back two thousand years. Some Egyptian hieroglyphs show men holding electrical devices that look like giant light bulbs. There's no evidence of soot on the walls of the temples housing the hieroglyphs, so how did they make them in dark spaces without light? There's this thingamabob called the Antikythera Mechanism they found in 1900, it's like a clock full of bronze gears and it predicts eclipses and stuff. Thing is, it's two-thousand years old. Scientists find way too many things like that for us to believe we're

the most advanced civilization that ever
lived. We're being lied to."

"How do you know all this?"

"I told you. I'm gonna be an archeologist."

"Still?"

"Yeah."

He seemed disappointed, but conceded,
"You'd be good at that."

"Thanks," I beamed. "Anyway, all the
stories about Atlantis mention advanced
technology. Some even blame technology
for its downfall. They say the Atlanteans
blew themselves up, or angered the gods
somehow. So, it isn't all that surprising if
Kara has outrageous abilities."

"Her abilities take some getting used to,"
Bo said, embarrassed by the way he reacted.

"I peed my pants the first time I saw her."

He shoved my shoulder and laughed,
"You're just saying that."

Knowing we could talk to Kara any time
we wanted, we put the incident behind us. I
told Bo about my visit with Mrs. Dunaway.
He listened without interrupting and I
watched his eyes pool up as I described her
pain and angst. By the time I finished, we
were both on the edge of tears. Then I told

B.K. Crawford

him about my nightmare and that seemed to light a fire in him.

"As soon as we got that list from the library, I asked my Aunt Emily to check the names I remembered against the register at the church. One of them was buried there last year."

"Holy socks," I groaned, "why didn't you tell me right away?"

"Because I thought we learned to leave the dead alone after what we did to Davey Newhouse at the church."

"After what *you* did," I corrected him. "Bo, we need to know if that victim died without his eyes or not."

"That's all we need to know, just that one little thing?"

"Don't be sarcastic. If we can find some truth in what Mrs. Dunaway said, we'll know there's a good chance she told the truth about everything."

He looked at me like I'd dropped my last marble. "So, we just go to the cemetery, dig this kid up, then waltz home for a root beer float?"

"Do you have a better idea?"

Shifting his weight on the hay bale, he turned away to avoid eye contact and did a

B.K. Crawford

lot of heavy sighing. When he finally spoke, he sounded squeamish, "Wouldn't the eyes be decomposed after a year, anyway?"

"It doesn't matter. If he died without them, the undertaker would pack the sockets with marbles or gauze to make them look like they were still there."

"Dang, you know some gruesome things," he groaned.

"It's what archeologists do. So, what do you say? Are you up for some grave robbing, or not?"

He scratched his head and gave it some thought. "If I say no, what will you do?"

I didn't hesitate, "Go by myself."

He dropped his chin to his chest in defeat. "All right. When and where?"

"Meet me at my place at eleven tonight. My parents should be asleep by then. If they aren't, I'll flash the lights in my room so you'll know to wait a little longer. Deal?"

He offered a slow, reluctant nod. "I'll do the digging, you do the examining," he insisted.

I bumped his shoulder with mine and smiled. We'd get to the bottom of this mystery yet.

B.K. Crawford

Snipping Threads
ВЖВ

Momma and Daddy were asleep by ten-thirty, so by the time Bo showed up at my place, I stood waiting on the road by the mailbox.

Another in a string of hot summer nights, the humidity clung so tightly we couldn't tell if we were sweating, or if the night air was pearling off our skin. Not the best conditions for a bout of heavy digging. I'd packed extra watermelon ale and a jug of water, assuming we'd need every drop. Bo had a good sized shovel strapped to his back, a crowbar in his pocket, and a large canteen of his own.

We walked with our flashlight beams directed at the ground so we wouldn't stumble on the rocks and ruts in the road and to avoid the prying eyes of scattered neighbors who had nothing better to do than to peer out their windows all night in search of gossip fodder. As an added precaution, we turned our flashlights off altogether when we approached houses with lights still twinkling in their windows.

We listened as the crickets and frogs sang odes to the high humidity, which seemed to

B.K. Crawford

be cause for a grand celebration among their kind, their songs especially loud and boisterous.

The smell of freshly turned manure hung like a blanket in the air, unyielding.

"It's gonna rain," Bo whispered.

"Mmm," I grunted, "Hopefully not before we finish."

We arrived at the cemetery, unscathed, but drenched in sweat.

There, we searched headstones for the name of the unfortunate victim, Marcus Stoddard. After half an hour of searching in vain, we stopped.

"Are you sure that's the name on the list?" I asked.

"Absolutely."

"And you're sure he's buried here, in this cemetery?"

"My Aunt Emily works here, it's the only church register she checked. He has to be here."

"We've read every stone from north to south," I mumbled. Then it occurred to me that maybe we weren't looking for a stone. I swung my flashlight beam over the grounds and noted several mausoleums.

B.K. Crawford

"Come on." I led Bo to the first mausoleum and shined a light on the name over the door. *Dexter Bradford, 1908-1944.*

Three other mausoleums were also unhelpful, but the fourth one read: *Marcus Stoddard, 1958-1962.*

Bingo.

In reverence, we stood in silence, grieving for the fallen little man of four.

Then Bo proclaimed, "My work is done."

"What?"

"I dig, you examine. We made a deal."

"How do we open this door?" I asked, shining my light beam on a strangely ornamented door handle.

Reaching out, Bo gripped the handle, moving it up and to the right like a gear shift. A metallic click indicated success. Pulling with a grunt, Bo opened the door and stepped back to allow me through.

"Ladies first."

I walked past Bo and took a quick inventory of the dreary tomb. The crypt walls stood high, but there wasn't much room inside, barely enough for Bo and me to stand side by side. Sticky cobwebs molested us and the air smelled of spoiled potatoes, sour and clammy—the scent of expired time.

B.K. Crawford

Before us, a tiny casket sat atop a marble slab, covered in webs and dust.

"Can I have the crowbar?"

Bo pulled the tool from his back pocket. "Step aside, little Lady," he said, wiping a string of cobwebs off the coffin lid.

Moments later, he'd managed to pry the hinges, but refused to open the lid for fear he might topple another casket.

"Hold the flashlight," I instructed, and slowly lifted the lid.

The body looked so small, so shriveled, like a discarded doll in a forgotten attic. Wisps of light hair grew around the boy's face and his fingernails had also grown freakishly long. Swallowing hard, I fought to keep from shaking and reminded myself why we were here.

I reached into my field bag and took out a pair of scissors.

"Stand beside me, Bo. But don't look inside."

Bo edged closer and I grabbed his hand, positioning the light where I needed it. "That's good. Hold it right there."

The quivering light beam gave Bo's frazzled nerves away. I needed to finish and get out as fast as possible. Leaning over the

B.K. Crawford

edge of the casket, I moved strands of wayward hair away from the boy's eyes and located the stitches holding his eyelids in place. I snipped the threads on the left eye, one by one, and carefully lifted the brittle eyelid.

Dropping my scissors, I gasped. *Gauze*.

It would seem Mrs. Dunaway had told me true.

Marcus Stoddard had no eyes.

We did our best to restore the crypt to its original state, minus the snipped eyelid and broken hinges.

"It could be a coincidence," Bo mumbled as we pointed our light beams at the ground, zigzagging around tombstones on our way out of the cemetery.

"I guess it could," I said, not convinced, my face growing hot with broiling anger.

How could anyone do such a thing to little children? Who could have such a bitter soul? Or, had soulless demons done these things, as Mrs. Dunaway claimed?

It seemed as though the heavens mirrored my mood when a bolt of lightning cracked against the sky and heavy rain began to pelt us.

B.K. Crawford

Murder on Moon Street

We ran for the cover of the trees on the side of the road, but it didn't help much. In less than thirty seconds, we were soaked to the gills and dripping.

"Look," Bo said, pointing off in the distance.

I could barely see through the blur as warm sheets of water poured over my eyes. Blinking rapidly, I followed Bo's outstretched arm to see a white orb, glowing profusely, hovering over the tips of the trees to the east. The glow reminded me of Kara and I reached for my field bag, squeezing until I felt her crystals inside.

Tromping through mud puddles, we ran, looking up now and then to find the orb still hovering over the trees. It didn't move, it made no sound, but hovered there in its throbbing glow like a misplaced star.

"What the hell is it?" Bo barked, and my arm hair might have stood on end if it wasn't sopping wet. Grabbing him by the hand, I yanked, drawing him further away from the road and deeper into the woods.

Somewhere nearby, there stood an old hunting shack my brothers used to use. If we couldn't find the shack, then maybe a hollow

B.K. Crawford

log, or a small cave—anything to shield us from the storm and the menacing orb.

Our flashlight beams bounced erratically as we ran, illuminating tree trunks, mossy stones, fallen twigs and, ultimately, a ragged red bandana tied around a birch trunk.

"*Stop*," I screamed, slipping to a sudden halt.

"What's wrong?" The abrupt stop knocked him off his feet.

Helping him up, I pointed to the bandana. "Hunters use those as a warning."

"For what?"

"Bear traps."

Bo's eyes went wide. "What do we do?"

"Grab a long stick," I said, frantic, searching for a sufficient specimen myself, not finding anything in the immediate area.

"Hold my flashlight." He handed it to me and unsnapped the sheath of a bowie knife he wore on his belt. Climbing the closest tree, he cut two long, thin branches. Once they fell, I picked them up and waited for Bo to climb back down.

"The light's still there," he reported, recovering his flashlight. "Maybe it's a helicopter."

B.K. Crawford

"Helicopters are noisy. Don't move without testing the ground with your stick first." I jabbed the ground with my stick, taking tentative steps.

Bo carefully imitated me. We'd only gone a few yards when a bear trap snapped and ate the bottom of his stick. He dropped his flashlight and screeched like a banshee. I would have done the same.

"This isn't safe," he shouted, "We gotta get back to the road."

I didn't have time to respond because the sun suddenly appeared, bathing us in a bright, white light. Or, so it seemed until I realized it couldn't have been any later than midnight.

Looking up, we found the silent orb pulsing directly over our heads.

I turned to see the fear in Bo's eyes. "Don't run. *Bear traps*."

Stuck, we stood still, hand-in-hand, hoping the light would go away. Cornered like two mice caught in a vat of peanut butter, we dropped to our knees and quivered.

Things got a little wonky from there on and I don't like to talk about what happened next. I've heard there are remote hospitals, hidden deep in the hills, where they keep

B.K. Crawford

white jackets with strong zippers and locks on long sleeves for people who talk about things no one can possibly believe. I've also heard too much adrenaline can bring on hallucinations and that's just as good an explanation as anything else. Still, I'll call up some courage and tell it the way I remember it.

Bo and me crouched in the middle of the blinding light, stuck with nowhere to go, his hand clutching mine so hard it's a wonder he didn't break every bone. Then, a pale blue beam of light came from the center of the orb and picked Bo off the ground like a flimsy piece of paper, drawing him up into the belly of the orb. He screamed my name every inch of the way. I reached for him, but he left the ground so fast, I couldn't catch him. My shrieking blended with his.

I felt helpless, frenzied, sick to my stomach, confused and, worst of all, responsible. There had to be some way to get Bo back, but I couldn't imagine what to do. So, I raised my eyes to the orb and threatened it with God's wrath if it didn't let him go.

Darkness.

Complete.

B.K. Crawford

I saw the orb there one minute, then lost sight of it in a fraction of a second.

I couldn't feel the forest floor under my feet anymore. I didn't hear the croaking of the frogs or the chirping of the crickets. I couldn't smell the rain or taste it on my lips. For the longest time, I couldn't move at all and I wondered—Am I dead?

I came to my senses when a stream of sunlight broke through my bedroom window and warmly embraced my face. I had no memory of walking home. Tugging on my pajamas, I wondered who had put them on.

"Jennifer Jane Houston," Momma yelled, "Now, or no breakfast."

Sitting up, I tried to get my bearings.

Bo. Where's Bo? I had to get help.

Throwing my pajamas off, I dressed in a rush and thumped down the stairs.

On my way to the kitchen, the phone rang, so I stopped to pick it up.

"J.J.?"

"Bo? Where are you?"

"I woke up in bed. You okay?"

"I'm fine. Holy socks, what happened?"

Silence.

"I don't know," he mumbled. "Are you coming by today?"

B.K. Crawford

"I'll be there as soon as I can."

I hung up the phone, intending to get to Bo as quick as possible.

Not hungry, I wolfed breakfast down so fast I don't remember what I ate. Placing my dishes in the sink, I turned to leave, but Momma had other ideas. Grabbing me by the shirttail, she told me to wash the dishes, mop the kitchen floor, run the vacuum cleaner in the living room, tidy up my bedroom and weed the garden before I did anything else. I opened my mouth to argue, but could see by the stern look on her face, I would only be wasting precious time.

The housekeeping went by in a flash, but there's no way to skimp on weeding without strays rearing their ugly heads. So, I set my back to the task, the morning sun already scorching. By the time I finished, my clothes were black with dirt and wet with sweat. In a rush, I changed clothes and finally made my escape.

I found Bo in the stable, brushing down Candy Girl, his mother's equestrian mare. Seeing me, he dropped the brush and left the stall, swatting bits of hay from his jeans as he locked the rail.

B.K. Crawford

"What took so long?" He asked, clearly tense.

I told him about the list of chores Momma dumped on me and he nodded, all too familiar with parental madness.

"I thought you weren't allowed in here," I muttered, remembering Bo's Momma had forbidden him to go anywhere near the stable after he set all the farm animals free a few years ago. The animals all came back for dinner, but Mrs. Duke lost her sanity for a few hours in the meantime.

Bo flicked a thumb toward Candy Girl, "Seems I've been forgiven."

"Shame your Dad didn't forbid you to go near the pigs," I joked.

"What happened to us last night?" Bo demanded, taking me by the arm, pulling me onto a wooden bench.

I recounted everything I remembered about him being lifted off the ground and sucked into the orb.

"I don't remember that." His expression was quizzical and concerned. "I remember seeing the light, then everything went fuzzy. I don't know how I got home."

"Me either."

B.K. Crawford

J. J. HOUSTON ℅252
Murder on Moon Street

"I've been thinking about it all morning. Maybe there were some embalming chemicals left in that kid in the crypt. Maybe we were hallucinating."

I certainly understood Bo's desire to chalk our experience up as unreal. I would have liked to believe the same. But, one thing stood out in my mind—I didn't think two people could hallucinate the same thing at the same time and I told him so.

"What happened then?"

Not sure, I didn't answer. We sat there, staring at each other, neither of us wanting to voice what we really thought. Aliens. Or, government posing as aliens. Or both.

Bo broke the silence. "What'd they do to us?"

I shrugged my shoulders and shook my head, lost for an answer.

"I might have something that belongs to them," I finally confessed.

"The crystals?"

"No, I don't think they care about Kara. But I did take that pair of goggles from the room at the end of the shaft. Remember?"

"Oh my God," Bo sputtered, "You have to give them back."

B.K. Crawford

"I don't know about you, but I don't think I want to go back. The fall wasn't exactly comfortable."

"So, throw them back down the hole. Jeez, J.J. They'll come back if you have something they want."

"What if it's not the goggles they want?" I moaned, "What if it's *us*. Maybe we're getting too close to the truth."

"Then stop. Forget about all of it."

I understood his fear and desperation, but I couldn't agree with his reasoning.

"If we stop, every time we read about another dead kid, we'll know we gave up. We'll know we could have done something to save a life."

"But, *we* could die."

I nodded. "But look at all we've been through so far and here we are, no worse for the wear."

"No worse? I'm scared out of my skull. We don't even remember how we got in bed."

"I'm scared, too. We might not remember how we got home, but we do know that's where we ended up. They didn't kill us. We're not dead. That has to mean something. Besides, giving up doesn't

B.K. Crawford

automatically mean they'll stop coming after us. We might already know too much. Like it, or not, this is where we are."

I could tell from the blank look on Bo's face I'd driven my point home.

"Then, let's get some help. We can tell someone."

"Who?"

"Our parents?"

"And, what can they do? If that thing can pick you up off the ground and wipe your memory clean, it can do the same to your father. And mine."

"The police?"

"You remember what Phoebe told us. There's a whole nest of them in on this," I said, absorbing the worried look on his face, understanding his frustration.

"It's all my fault. I'm sorry I dragged you into this. I had no idea. I won't ask you to do any more, I promise."

His eyes shifted while he thought it over.

"No. You're right," he said. "Giving up probably won't make a difference. If you're not gonna quit, then I won't either. But, no more traipsing around after dark. Agreed?"

"We'll be more careful from now on," I promised.

B.K. Crawford

"What's our next move?" Bo asked.

"Maybe it's time we learn more about Hank Hornbrook."

"How?"

"I don't know. Find out where he lives? Take a look around his place?"

"You mean, break in?"

B.K. Crawford

Breaking In
ВЖВ

Bo and I snooped until we found a card in Mr. Duke's directory indicating he delivers five pounds of fresh bacon, every month, to *H. Hornbrook, 33 Crow's Nest Road*. What's more, because of the remote location, Mr. Duke had drawn a simple line-map to help him make the delivery.

Bo and I stared at the card. Hornbrook's house sat on the outskirts of Sullivan swamp, nearly twenty-five miles from the Duke farm.

"It's too far," Bo grumbled, discouraged. "Ain't no way we'll get back in time for chores."

Disappointed, I had to agree, the trip would take too long. Even if we peddled without stopping, we still wouldn't have time to get home before dark. Red flags would go up everywhere and parents would fret; Daddy and Miss Tilly especially, both of them knowing there's a killer on the loose.

Miss Tilly. *That's it.*

"Bo? You told Miss Tilly you're a good driver. Is that true?"

"Sure. I'm on my Pop's tractor more than he is these days."

B.K. Crawford

"Not tractors. Cars."

"It's pretty much all the same...pedals, steering wheels and mirrors. Pop lets me drive the truck to pick up hay. Nothing to it. Why?"

"You're right, it's way too far to ride our bikes. What if we can get there faster?"

Bo cocked an eyebrow all stern and serious, "If you think I'm gonna steal my dad's truck..."

"No," I reassured him with a pat on the arm, "Miss Tilly's Dodge."

"You're gonna let her to drive us to Hank Hornbrook's place?"

I shook my head. After the trip to the library, neither of us wanted to get into a car with Miss Tilly again. "You said you can drive. We'll be there and back before she even knows the car is gone."

"We're planning to sneak off with your Grandmother's car?"

Nodding, I asked if he had a better idea.

"Yep. Skip the trip altogether."

"But, Hank Hornbrook is the biggest clue we have. We know he's involved. There's no question. If there's any evidence connecting him to the crimes, it's probably at his place. Tell me I'm wrong and I'll drop it."

B.K. Crawford

"You're talking about stealing a car."

A breath of frustration rippled over my lips. "We're not stealing, we're *borrowing*. Like I said, we'll be back before she knows the car is gone." Even as I spoke the words, I thought about Miss Tilly's uncanny ability to sense what's going on around her. But what choice did we have?

Bo took a deep breath filled with uncertainty. "You have a plan?"

I thought it over. "She likes to dance to loud music. You can start the car and get it out of the barn without her hearing. Drive it to the end of the road and wait for me. I'll join you once I'm done distracting her."

Thumb yanking on his belt loop, he leaned in. "Aren't you forgetting something?"

"What?"

"The keys?"

I grunted in frustration. It's always something.

I watched several scenarios play out in my mind until I'd convinced myself I could find a way. "I'll get the keys. After I have them, I'll make an excuse to go see Pappy in the outhouse and you can take the keys from there. Just don't rev the engine, get it out of the barn as quietly as you can."

B.K. Crawford

An hour later, I left Bo hiding behind Miss Tilly's outhouse and opened the screen door. She already had Kate Smith belting out a ballad at full volume. My lucky day.

"Miss J.J.," She squealed, grabbing my shoulders and pulling me in for a hug.

She wore a black hat with ebony netting, the brim of the hat cocked over her brow so that I could barely see her eyes. I didn't recognize this get-up, she'd never worn it before.

"Who are you today?

She snorted, as if it should've been obvious, "Mata Hari."

"A spy?"

"The Queen is in need of information," she whispered, releasing me and turning toward the refrigerator. She bent to pull out a brown sack and handed it to me.

"Your lunch," she announced, closing the refrigerator door. Then she went to the sink and reached for a tin perched on a shelf overhead. Struggling with the lid, she popped it open and handed me her car keys.

"Have it back before dark. Now, go. You don't have all day."

B.K. Crawford

Jaw unhinged, I stared at her. She put the keys in the palm of my hand and wrapped my fingers around them.

"Go on. And be careful. Tell your muddy boyfriend cars aren't toys."

Slapping me on the rump, she moved me toward the door. Head twisted over my shoulder, I couldn't stop staring at her.

"Back before dark," she repeated, nearly pushing me out the door.

"You're only saying that so I won't feel bad about stealing a car," Bo accused when I told him what Miss Tilly had done.

"Really? Then where'd I get this bag of sandwiches?" I rattled the bag in his face, waiting for a reply.

With nothing to say, he turned the key in the ignition and nudged the Dodge out of the barn.

Pulling the car onto the road like a practiced expert, Bo conceded, "She really just let you have the keys?"

"Yep, and she said to tell you cars ain't toys."

"Of course they're not," he huffed.

Oddly, I felt all grown up sitting in the seat beside Bo while he navigated the dirt roads

B.K. Crawford

that would lead us to Hank Hornbrook's place.

"Do you feel old?" I asked, rolling the window down, hoping for cooler air.

"No. Should I?"

"You're driving a car."

He chuckled. "I've been doing this since I could see over the steering wheel. It's nothing new."

"I've never seen you drive before. You're good at it. I feel safe. Not like when Miss Tilly drives."

"She's a nightmare," he laughed. "It's not so hard if you're taught to do it right."

"Will you teach me?"

He quickly scanned his mirrors then looked to me. "Not today," he said, returning his focus to the road ahead.

"No, not today," I mumbled, somewhat disappointed. We had more important things to do.

When we arrived, we drove past Hank's house several times, watching closely, checking for any sign of movement, any indication he might be home. Mostly convinced no one lurked inside, we parked the car off-road about an eighth of a mile from the house and walked.

B.K. Crawford

J. J. HOUSTON ©262
Murder on Moon Street

As soon as we got out of the car, the bitter stench of swamp gas assaulted us—it smelled like a wicked cloud of ceaseless diarrhea hanging thick in the air. Crows and vultures fought a feather-raising battle over some dead thing in the marsh, their loud, ornery caws clawing down my spine until I felt as though my nerve might escape through bleeding ears. Clearly, this land had suffered a tragic death.

We approached the house with all the stealth we could muster, hiding behind tree stumps, using tall grass for cover, light on our feet, and speaking with an occasional whisper.

We saw no lights on, but didn't expect to see those in full daylight anyway.

As we skirted around the house, peeking in the windows, we fought to suppress nagging coughs inspired by the overwhelming stink.

The house, a ranch style home, seemed nice enough, not a mansion, but no shanty either. It had paint and a porch, window shutters and empty flower boxes, and a neatly groomed yard, despite the grass growing gray. Hornbrook gave the place enough attention to indicate he had money

B.K. Crawford

to spend. But, how anyone could live so close to the swamp, subjected to the smell of that horrid gas, I couldn't imagine. Truly nasty, the air smelled almost as bad as Davey Newhouse's rotting corpse.

"I suppose you get used to it, after a while," Bo retched.

"Don't barf," I whispered, wishing I had something pleasant to sniff.

As I watched a vulture tear the feathers off a small crow, I realized I couldn't think of a more perfect place to hide the bodies of missing children than right there in the middle of Sullivan swamp. Unnerved by the thought, I focused on following Bo around the house.

A couple outbuildings stood in the back—a barn big enough to hold a tractor or two and a small shed. We found the front and back doors locked, but Bo managed to lift the door on the bulkhead leading to the basement.

He pulled a small flashlight from his pocket. "This way." I reckon he would've made a good Boy Scout.

Dark and damp with a dirt floor, the basement had a low ceiling and a musty scent. Hank had scattered boxes here and there—broken dishes, old magazines, faded photographs, nothing interesting. We inspected a few shelves, but only found tools and useless pieces of hardware. Moldy cushions from discarded furniture blossomed in dark corners.

Not a single cowboy hung chained to the wall.

We snooped around for a few minutes but got bored when we found nothing out of the ordinary.

"The stairs are over here," Bo whispered and we climbed them, very slowly, so as not to make a sound.

The basement door opened into the kitchen. Apparently, Hank spent all his free time on the exterior of the house and left the inside to rot. Dirty dishes piled up in the sink, pots and pans full of grease sat on the stove, bottles and cans lined up the counters—an absolute smorgasbord for the army of ants scampering away with sugar crystals and bread crumbs.

I won't even say what kind of mess we found in the bathroom, but the stink outdid the swamp gas ten-to-one. Holding our noses, we backed out and closed the door behind us.

B.K. Crawford

"I'd let my bladder pop before I'd sit on that toilet," I vowed.

In the next room, we figured a bed probably lived somewhere under a massive mound of dirty laundry.

"Guy needs a wife," Bo snorted.

"Cruel and unusual punishment," I countered. "He needs a backhoe and a box of matches. Check the closet."

The door creaked when Bo opened it and I held my breath because it made the loudest noise since we came in.

Bo yanked on a long piece of string dangling from the ceiling and a dim light switched on. Several starched suits hung front and center, along with three pair of shiny shoes lined up on a shelf just off the floor. Hank's work clothes. Hangers screeched against the metal rod as Bo pushed the suits aside, inspecting shirts and ties until he uncovered what we expected to find. Hidden in the shadows, on the right-hand side of the closet, hung a brown suede man-sized cowboy suit, rhinestones and all.

Tearing the suit from the hanger, Bo flung it at me. "There it is, let's go."

"What?" I asked, confused.

B.K. Crawford

"We found the cowboy outfit. We're done."

"But..."

"No, buts, J.J.," he barked, pushing past me on his way back to the kitchen.

"Wait," I called after him, louder than I would've liked. "It's not illegal to own a cowboy outfit. This doesn't prove anything."

He stopped and turned to face me, anger mixing with fear in his glare.

"Then, what are we looking for?"

I stared at the rhinestones on the lapel of the shirt in my hands. "I'm not sure, but maybe a record...a list. Something to connect him to the victims. Chains maybe? I don't know."

"We're standing inside a strange man's house...a killer...and you don't know? What we're doing is against the law. You don't *know*?"

I felt my face flush. "It won't help to get mad at each other. But you're right, it's against the law. So, let's do what we have to do as quickly as we can and get out. We need to split up. You go to the outbuildings, see if you can find anything. I'll look through the paperwork in the house. We'll meet at the car in half an hour, okay?"

B.K. Crawford

Bo shook his head. "I don't like the idea of splitting up."

"It'll take twice as long if we don't."

Reluctant, he stared at me, unsure. "All right, but take this." He unhooked his hunting knife and handed it to me. "Strap it on your belt and use it if you have to."

Nodding, I put it on.

"Don't mess around, J.J."

I promised I wouldn't dawdle. Bo left through the back door and I took the cowboy outfit back to the bedroom.

After returning the outfit, I left the bedroom and noticed a short door at the end of the hallway. Curious, I tugged on the knob. Locked. Wondering why Hank would keep a door locked inside his own home, a burst of excitement ran through me. Mounds of evidence might lurk behind that door. Then I noticed a key dangling from the keyhole beneath the door knob. Oh.

Turning the key, I opened the door and ducked inside the dark hollow. I stood before a thin stairwell leading to the attic. It seemed as good a place as any to start.

The wooden slats beneath my feet creaked in defiance as I ascended.

B.K. Crawford

Steamed air swelled so hot in the attic I could smell the timbers baking. My eyes adjusted in the darkness. Hank had a large desk and several cabinets perched against a far wall. A banker's lamp sat on the desk, so I tugged the chain and the light came on. No cobwebs, very little dust, and the paperwork spread over the surface of the desk looked like Hank put it there recently. He must use the attic a lot. My heartbeat increased.

Bending over the desk, I flipped through memos from the state house, a few pieces of bundled legislature, and bills of lading for office supplies. A receipt for one hundred bags of lye caught my attention. Fifty pounds each. I remembered a detective in one of Daddy's television shows saying lye speeds up decomposition; it's a serial killer's best friend. I folded the invoice and stuffed it in my pocket, knowing I hadn't found enough evidence. Obviously, lye has other uses as well, like making soap. Hank might've bought the lye for his sister, Phoebe. And, if he didn't, he would surely claim he had. I needed more.

I found nothing else of interest on the desk, so I rummaged through the drawers until I came to a lower compartment that

B.K. Crawford

wouldn't budge. This time, I couldn't locate a key. Maybe if I thumped it with a knee, it would pop open. Nope. With no time to mull it over, I used Bo's Bowie knife to break the lock.

Now Hank wouldn't have to wonder if someone had broken in, he would know for sure. Broken wood shards littered the floor and the lock would never work again.

Trembling, I plunged my hands into the drawer and lifted files onto the top of the desk. Scanning the papers, I read as fast as possible. Life Insurance policies, the deed to his car, home insurance, utility bills, tax returns, receipts from a shopping catalog for twenty-five cowboy costumes—size five to fifteen. Bingo.

Once again, I reminded myself it's not against the law to buy clothes. I sorted through the whole stack of files and found nothing else of interest. As I reached to stuff the files back into the drawer, I saw something I'd missed before—a metal lock box. Dropping the files on the floor, I took the box from the drawer and went to work on the lock with Bo's knife. By the time it opened, I'd created another mangled mess. But it held an invaluable treasure. The list of

B.K. Crawford

children's names printed in Hank's secret ledger would match the obituaries for the last five years, name-for-name, I felt sure of it. Stuffing the ledger under my shirt and into my waistband, I nearly flew down the stairs.

I don't remember opening my mouth, but my ears registered a loud-pitched scream I recognized as my own.

Hank Hornbrook stood waiting for me at the bottom of the stairs, arms outstretched, his gnarly hands reaching for my throat. Momentum threw me into his arms. Dragging me from the stairwell, he threw me to the floor, straddled my stomach, and pinned my shoulders to the floor, his face purple with explosive rage. I expelled another unprompted scream and he took me by the throat.

"Nosy little brat, you've got some nerve." The spittle from his lips landed on my face. "Who sent you? Who you working for?"

My fingers stretched out, searching for Bo's knife, as I kicked and screamed, struggling against the old man's weight. Frantic, I patted around my waist, but couldn't feel the knife handle. Had I lost the knife when I fell, or did I forget to put it back in its sheath when I opened the lock-box?

B.K. Crawford

Increasing pressure on my throat, Hank growled, "Tell me, or I'll choke the life out of you."

I found it almost impossible to speak with his fingers pressing into my throat. "I'm not working for anybody," I managed to say.

"Liar," he spat, the color in his face darkening. "I've seen them snooping around." He squeezed harder and I began to see sparkles of light swimming in my vision.

"Why'd you kill all those kids?" I gurgled.

Kicking wildly, I lifted my hips and ran my hand around my back, hoping to find the knife there. The sheath must have slipped around my waist when I fell because I felt the knife handle just above my right hip.

"I never killed no kids," he snarled, "Until now."

Wrapping my fingers around the knife handle, I slipped the knife from the sheath and gripped it with all my might. Remembering what Hank's sister, Phoebe, told me and Bo about Hank throwing cats into barn fans, I didn't believe him. I stared into his cruel eyes and wondered if I could live with myself once I'd killed a man.

I didn't have long to wonder.

B.K. Crawford

J. J. HOUSTON ℅272
Murder on Moon Street

The expression in Hank's squinted eyes went from cruel to pure evil as he increased the pressure on my neck one-hundred fold and I knew in that moment, he had committed in his soul to kill me.

I lifted the knife into position, prepared to plunge the blade in his back, when I heard a strange heavy metallic thud. Hank's eyes rolled back, his head lolled to the side, and he fell, full weight, onto my chest, unconscious.

"Are you all right?" Bo roared, dropping a cast iron frying pan onto the floor.

"Get him off," I wailed.

Bo grabbed Hank by the shoulders and practically threw the old man through an adjacent wall.

He helped me to my feet, staring at the naked blade in my hand.

"Cripes," he huffed, prying the knife from my hand, moving me down the hall, away from Hank's crumpled form and into the living room.

"Where'd he come from?"

Taking me in his arms, Bo hugged me tight. "I was in the shed when I heard a car pull into the driveway. I came as quick as I could."

"Thank God," I whispered.

B.K. Crawford

If Bo hadn't shown up when he did, I would have been dead or soaked in Hank Hornbrook's blood. Someday, I'd have to find a way to thank him for saving me from those dreadful possibilities, but we needed to get out of the house and back to the car.

Bo suddenly pushed me so hard I almost tripped over a coffee table. By the time I recovered my bearings and turned around, I saw Hank Hornbrook stumbling down the hall toward Bo with the frying pan held high over his head. Bo stood his ground, knife pointed menacingly in Hank's direction.

The fight remains an anxious stain on my memory. Like a slow dance, they circled one another while I continuously moved out of the way; Hank swinging the frying pan and missing, Bo jabbing air with his knife. They went round and round until Hank decided to take the high ground by jumping onto the coffee table. Lifting the frying pan with both hands, he meant to bring it crashing down on Bo's head but, in mid swing, the pan smashed into a light fixture instead. We heard glass shatter, then loud popping noises. An acrid stink spread as fire chewed wires and sparked out of the fixture, catching in Hank's hair and settling into the fibers of his jacket.

B.K. Crawford

J. J. HOUSTON c274
Murder on Moon Street

Dropping the frying pan, he howled and
slapped at his head, trying to put the fire out.
Seeing his dilemma as the perfect distraction,
Bo and me ran from the house and made our
way back to Miss Tilly's Dodge.

B.K. Crawford

Goners

ВЖВ

Expressing my penance to the Lord God High Almighty, I thanked Him for allowing Bo and me to escape Hank Hornbrook's house with our lives. As an added bonus, I begged Him to save me from Bo's heavy foot.

Miss Tilly's Dodge threw a cloud of dust high over the trees as Bo tore down the road, boot to the floor. We hit ruts so deep, we popped off the vinyl seat and smacked our heads on the roof of the car. I wished I'd buckled the seat belt.

No way under the sun would I criticize Bo's driving after the way he'd saved my life and I certainly understood his sense of urgency in getting us as far away from Hank Hornbrook as possible. Still, I worried about making it home in one piece and I worried about the car. Several sharp curves in the road turned us into human pin balls, bouncing into and off of one another.

Once we got a few miles away from Hank's place, Bo would lighten up on the gas, or so I hoped.

We were whipping around a wide turn in the road when a car tore out of the trees

B.K. Crawford

behind us. Gazing over my shoulder, I saw a black and white police car, following in hot pursuit, siren screaming.

"Cops," I said, as if Bo hadn't already heard the blaring siren.

For a minute there, I thought we were goners. We'd pull over, the cops would put us in handcuffs and cart us off to the station where they'd book us for reckless driving, breaking and entering, assault, and arson. But the Dodge lunged forward with more speed than before.

"What are you doing?"

Wide-eyed, Bo shot a glance at me, "I ain't got a license."

"Bo..." I started, but the cop nudged our back bumper, sending us into a slight skid.

"Prick," Bo mumbled, jerking the car back in line with the road. "Hold on J.J., we're going for a ride."

Hold on to what, I wondered, pretty sure we had already gone for the wildest ride in my recollection.

Bo let off the gas slightly and slowed, which confused me. But, once the cop raced up and locked onto our bumper, Bo tromped on the gas again and made a sharp right, heading for a wooden fence that stood guard

B.K. Crawford

over a hilly pasture. Because Bo made his turn so fast, the cop car took to spinning in circles. I shrieked as we crashed through the wooden gate and turned around just in time to watch the cop car end up nose first in the trunk of a tree.

And he says *I'm* dangerous.

We practically flew across the pasture, spooking a small herd of cows and a brood of turkeys along the way. The car moaned and groaned as it hopped over one bump after another and I worried about what Miss Tilly would say if we brought her car back in a body bag. The pasture turned into a steep slope and we climbed, Bo's foot to the floor, me still searching in vain for something to hold onto while we bounced around like two hot kernels in a popcorn kettle.

When we finally reached the top of the hill, we ended up barreling down a logging road that wound through a thick forest.

"Great," I muttered, "Now we're lost."

"Nope."

I took that to mean he knew where we were. Turned out, he did. The wooden gate, the pasture, the cows and the turkeys belonged to his uncle, George. Bo said he'd

B.K. Crawford

call about the broken gate and build a new one as soon as he could.

A few miles later, we were headed back to Moon Street where Bo finally felt comfortable enough to let up on the gas. He flipped a switch and we watched the wipers push turkey feathers off the windshield.

My breathing slowed and my heart rate returned to normal. I looked at Bo, watching his eyes work the road and the mirrors, wondering how a young boy could become such a gallant man overnight. So strong, so smart, so ready to take on the world. Maybe I didn't know him as well as I thought and never gave him the credit he deserved.

While I mulled it over, Bo hit the brakes, nearly sending my head into the dashboard. A big black Buick had lurched onto the road, cutting us off. With trees lining the road left and right, our only escape lay behind us. By the time Bo shifted the car into reverse, Lieutenant Shafer had already begun to pound on his window, demanding he roll it down. She held a pistol in her right hand, pointed right at us.

Goners. Goners for sure.

B.K. Crawford

Bo did as she asked. Gripping the door, she bent to look inside and saw me sitting in the passenger seat.

"I told you to leave this to the professionals," she spat, madder than a one-winged hornet, staring me down. "Once you're dead, there's no coming back. If I catch you two nosing around again, I'll lock you up for your own protection. Do I make myself clear?"

We both nodded until she seemed satisfied. Slapping Bo's door, she huffed off. Halfway back to her car, she holstered her pistol and grumbled, "God *damn* it."

She got back in her car, slammed the door in a fit and left.

Me and Bo sat there, staring at each other, totally confused. Once again, I felt lucky to be alive. I still believed the Lieutenant was a mole and I said as much to Bo. He didn't seem so sure.

"If she isn't with them, why didn't she arrest us? And what are the police doing all the way out here in the boonies to begin with?"

Bo gave me a stiff shrug for an answer.

B.K. Crawford

We made it home in one piece, but not the least bit happy about the dirt and turkey feathers plastered on her car, Miss Tilly gifted us with two pails of hot soapy water and some sponges.

B.K. Crawford

Our Next Move

ВЖВ

I went home good and tired that night. So tired, in fact, I forgot all about Hank's ledger until it came time to take my bath. I hadn't even thought to mention it to Bo while we slopped the hogs at his place. I considered dialing him up on the phone but decided he'd been through enough for one day. I'd fill him in later.

The hot bath water felt especially good as I washed the anxious events of the day off my skin and climbed into my pajamas.

Before I got into bed, I checked a few names in Hank's ledger against the list we'd taken from the library. Sure enough, they matched. Convinced Bo and me hadn't risked our lives for nothing, I tucked the ledger into my field bag and locked the closet door for good measure.

I slept like a drugged rock.

After breakfast the next morning, I phoned Bo, told him about the ledger and asked if he wanted to get together to plan our next move.

B.K. Crawford

"It'll have to wait a couple days," he moaned, "I've got a family re-union this weekend. Won't be back until Monday."

"Oh." I breathed a heavy sigh.

"Listen, I know you're a big girl who can take care of herself, but we've been through a lot this week. I'm gonna ask you, as a friend, to let it go until I get back. Don't go snooping around on your own. Did you see the newspaper?"

"Not yet, why?"

"Go look."

I set the phone down and grabbed the newspaper off the kitchen table. Front page, pictures and all, Hank Hornbrook's house had burned to the ground, his whereabouts, unknown.

"Oh my God," I whispered as I put the phone back to my ear. "Do you think he burned in the fire?"

"Hard to say. But, if he did or he didn't, it's no good. You understand?"

I let that sink in. "Yeah, I get it."

Bo took a deep breath and sighed, "Give the bee's nest a couple days to settle. Please, J.J., I'm begging."

B.K. Crawford

I told him not to worry and hung up, disappointed with losing my partner in mischief for a whole weekend.

The creek ran low after a couple weeks of hot sun. I sat on the bank watching strands of bright green mermaid hair rise and fall with the current. Birds flitted from tree to tree, singing sweet melodies, basking in the sun, oblivious to the problems perplexing me.

My thoughts kept returning to the exchange I'd had with Hank when I asked him why he'd killed those kids. His gnarly-faced expression made me believe he thought I had a screw loose, then he claimed he never killed anyone. He also said he'd seen someone snooping around his house, someone besides Bo and me. Who? And, why? Did someone else suspect him of foul play? The police car that tore out after us was parked near Hank's house and Lt. Shafer had obviously been close by as well. She threatened to lock us up for our own good. Why? Was I mistaken about her being on the wrong side of the law? She let us go when she clearly knew we'd broken into Hank's house. Isn't it a police officer's duty to arrest people who break the law? She hadn't said boo after seeing me leave the church where

B.K. Crawford

Bo spilled Davey Newhouse's remains all over the floor. Since she hadn't done her civil duty, I could only conclude she had a hand in helping to cover up for the killers. Right?

Untying my sneakers, I yanked them off and stuck my toes into the cold spring water.

Phoebe Hornbrook said a nest of evil lurked among government officials. Someone at the police department warned Hank Hornbrook when Daddy called to report the body. Mrs. Dunaway insisted a force bigger than all of us existed because eyeball-stealing, soul-sucking aliens were involved— the gods. Even after watching the glowing orb suck Bo into its belly the other night, I couldn't justify a belief in aliens. I had to search until I found a more rational reason behind everything. Right?

I had Hank Hornbrook's ledger. The names matched up with the victims. His involvement seemed cemented now. But, I doubted a man could kill eight hundred boys a year, spread out over sixty-seven counties, and keep it hidden all by himself. Someone, or something else had to be involved. So, who could I trust with the ledger? The government? The police? Daddy?

B.K. Crawford

Not ready to make a full confession to Daddy, I decided I still needed more to go on. That's when I realized mausoleums don't come cheap—only rich folks can afford the luxury. Since most of the victims came from families connected to government in one way or another, some of them had excellent finances. So, maybe I'd find more victims buried in the mausoleums at the cemetery. Bo said one kid buried without his eyes might be a coincidence, but what if there were more? If I could establish a pattern, would it help?

I'd made up my mind. Despite promising Bo we wouldn't go out after dark anymore, I decided to return to the cemetery on my own to see what I might find.

B.K. Crawford

J. J. HOUSTON ©286
Murder on Moon Street

No Way Out
ВЖВ

After the incident with the police, I remained on guard about who might have the local roads in their sights, so I walked behind the tree line on my way to the cemetery as much as possible. A bright moon lit my path while the crickets and toads belted out their romantic serenades.

My field bag hung heavy on my back, full of grave-robbing tools and the rest of my gear.

I removed a small flashlight from the bag (the smaller the beam, the less chance of detection) and twisted past tombstones, quietly approaching a nest of mausoleums.

A twig snapped behind me.

Swinging the light beam around, I scanned the area. A mangy dog sat next to a nearby tombstone, smiling back at me, tongue lolling like I might have a juicy steak in my bag. Swallowing past the lump in my throat, I ignored the mutt and resumed my mission, searching until I found a small mausoleum holding the remains of a young boy. The placard read: *Winston Bennet 1951-1960.*

B.K. Crawford

Reaching for the door, I tugged, not expecting it to open. I figured I'd probably spend quite some time trying to jimmy the door, but I huffed and puffed until I managed to pull it open wide enough to allow access.

Much like the last crypt I inspected, this tomb had a repulsive rancid smell and thick cobwebs hanging in every corner.

Another twig snapped, closer this time.

You ain't getting my bologna sandwich, I thought, and moved closer to the stone casket perched on a marble pedestal. Getting the lid off this one would take some doing. The stone top had to weigh a ton and would pose quite a challenge. I wished for Bo's amazing muscles. Circling the pedestal, I shined my light on a nearly invisible crack beneath the casket lid, looking for the best place to insert the small crowbar I'd brought along. Then I heard a snort of laughter as the mausoleum door closed with a heavy thud.

"Let's see you get out of this one," I heard a gruff voice howl.

Pounding on the door, I pleaded, "Let me out!"

In response, I heard a latch drop into the lock. Frantically, I searched, but found no handles on the inside of the door.

B.K. Crawford

J. J. HOUSTON ©288
Murder on Moon Street

"That'll teach you to mind your own business. Burn my house down, will ya." Each word he grumbled grew dimmer as he walked away.

"Mr. Hornbrook," I begged, "Please don't leave me here!"

Ear pressed to the cold door, I strained to listen, but only the sound of the dog's whimpering and whining came back to me.

"Go get help, boy," I screamed, hoping the dog might understand. His persistent whimpering told me he hadn't.

I pushed on the door, knowing it was locked. I begged the dog for help, knowing it was stupid. I searched for windows, knowing there weren't any. I wondered how Hank knew where to find me, knowing I would have no answers.

The anxiety intensified until I felt like a sweating stick of dynamite, a bee stuck inside a jar, desperate for air, moonlight, freedom— knowing I couldn't have any of it.

I patted down the walls and looked for seams between the walls and floor, hoping for a tiny hole I might expand. Yelling and beating the walls with my crowbar until my hands went numb, I hoped someone could hear. Someone besides the stupid dog.

B.K. Crawford

Worst of all, my flashlight beam began to flicker.

Out of options, I accepted my fate, slipping to the floor in a crumple.

Cold and alone, deflated, exhausted, defeated.

No one would ever find me inside this cold, black tomb. Who would even think to look in such a god-awful place?

How ironic, I thought, to die in the company of a victim murdered by the same hand that had locked me inside the tomb.

Since I might take my last breath here anyway, I may as well find out if they laid Winston Bennet to rest without his eyes. I surveyed the crypt until my field bag appeared in the flashlight beam; I'd put it on the floor while I pounded the walls with the crowbar. I would grab my canteen, re-energize myself with a drink of watermelon juice, then try to get the casket lid open before the flashlight failed.

As my rusty luck would have it, the beam burned out only moments later.

The deepest black I've ever known enveloped me. Lifting my hand, I waved it in front of my face. No matter how much I waved, I couldn't see the slightest

B.K. Crawford

movement. Clearly, no light could enter this crypt. What if that meant no air could get in either? I gasped, afraid to entertain the thought any further.

No amount of slapping, cursing, or begging could get the flashlight to come back on. Desperate, I fumbled with it, twisting until I felt it come apart. I dropped the batteries and felt around until I retrieved them, placing them back into the flashlight, not knowing if I'd done it right. Apparently not.

Don't I have a guardian angel? I wondered. Someone to watch over me in times of trouble? No sooner had this thought crossed my mind when I felt a faint pressure on my right cheek, as if someone had gently touched me with the tip of their finger. Directly after, I felt the sensation of butterfly kisses moving over the same cheek. For a moment I actually considered I might not be alone—God had sent an angel to come sit with me on the crypt's cold, stone floor. Then I felt a burning sting and realized I'd been bitten by a spider. Screaming, I jumped to my feet, slapping my face until I convinced myself I'd killed the sinister beast, then beat my head for good measure, afraid relatives had come to nest in my hair.

B.K. Crawford

I'd become disoriented in my frenzy. Arms spread wide, I twisted and turned until I located the marble pedestal before me. But, did the door to the crypt lie before me as well, or behind? Fingertips on the pedestal, I reached until I touched a wall but sensed only the cold, unable to tell the difference between the stone wall and the door. I remembered seeing my field bag on the floor; if I could locate it, I would have a better idea of my position.

Carefully lowering myself to hands and knees, I patted the floor, inching forward only when I felt sure I'd cleared the way. I sensed things beneath the palms of my hands, things I imagined as twigs, leaves, blades of grass, dead insects, and pebbles. This made for slow progress, as every object I encountered caused the memory of Miss Tilly's warning voice to repeat, *'Where one spider lives expect two.'*

Then came the eerie scratching noises, like nails on stone, sluggish scraping, stopping and starting at irregular intervals. Each time I heard the spooky sound, I'd stop to listen, stunting my exploration even further. I thought I heard a garbled voice growl, "Get

B.K. Crawford

out." I would have liked nothing better than to obey the voice's command. Cocking my head to the side, I listened for more, but couldn't hear anything past the fast thumping of my heart and anxious breathing.

After some time, I heard the scraping noises again. Was that the dog, or...? I didn't want to allow myself to wonder if Winston Bennet had become restless in his stale coffin.

My sense of time vanished with my sight. I can't say how long it took to find the field bag, it seemed like a double eternity, but I finally had it in my grip.

Fumbling to open the bag, I reached inside, feeling for the familiar shape of my canteen. My hand wrapped around a small box and, at first, I felt irritated at not finding the canteen right away, but suddenly realized what I held in my hand. Pulling the box from the bag, I practically tore it open, allowing the crystal lizard's green glow to fill the mausoleum.

I could see.

Yanking the other two boxes out of the bag, I kicked myself for not realizing I had an alternative light source with me all along. If

B.K. Crawford

what I had in mind worked, not only would I have light, but company as well.

Placing the crystals together, I watched as their colorful lights melded to become a brilliant white. Then the stones vibrated and lifted off the floor, doing their dance, mid-air. Soon, I saw Kara's welcoming smile and heard her say, "Hello, J.J."

Hologram, ghost, figment of my imagination—whatever—I have never been so happy to see another face.

I told her everything that happened since coming to the cemetery. She listened intently, asking questions when she didn't understand, offering words of comfort when she realized the extent of my dilemma.

"How awful," she exclaimed. "But, why would this man lock you in a tomb?"

I patiently told her everything—from finding Davey Newhouse's corpse to breaking into Hank's house.

"You've certainly had an interesting summer. I can see why they might want you out of the way. But you'll call your friend, Bo, and he'll come to get you."

"There's no telephone in here," I whimpered.

"You have your mind."

B.K. Crawford

I had no idea what she meant. "How does that help?"

"Telepathy," she said, like I should have come up with it on my own.

I shook my head and shrugged.

"You don't use telepathy?" Such doubt filled her remark, I felt too embarrassed to answer.

"Once, when I was little," she reminisced, "I went exploring. The sun shone so bright, the breeze so cool, I lost track of time and place and found myself hopelessly lost. So, I sat on a nearby rock and thought of my father, calling to him with my heart. He answered right away and asked me to show him my surroundings. I looked around, in every direction, soaking in the details to help him see what I saw. No sooner had I finished, when I saw him walking over a nearby hill, coming to rescue me."

"Wow."

She smiled. "Telepathy is so common among my people, it does no good to attempt to lie to our parents as they immediately sense guilt when it's present."

"Better you than me," I said.

"I find it sad to think such a talent no longer exists in your time. But, you are

B.K. Crawford

human. Surely, the ability remains, even if it might take some extra effort."

"I don't know," I mumbled, "I really don't think it'll work. Anyway, Bo is hundreds of miles away in Virginia."

"Your connection with him is heart-to-heart, no distance is great enough to sever it. What can it hurt to try?"

She did have a point and I had nothing better to do.

Kara guided me through the process by telling me to connect to Bo by allowing the way I felt about him when he's with me to permeate my entire being. Then we showed him my location by concentrating on the placard outside the mausoleum door with Winston Bennet's name on it. We repeated the ritual until my head began to loll, my eyelids growing heavy.

"You must sleep," Kara coaxed.

The thought provided a bit of a jolt.

"Here? In a grave?"

Kara chuckled.

"It's not funny," I shouted, "There's a dead boy in here."

"Please, forgive me. It's common among my people to sleep with the bones of our ancestors."

B.K. Crawford

"Well, it's frowned upon here, believe me."

"How sad. But, try looking at it this way. Man has thrived on Earth for millions of years. There isn't an inch of the planet upon which someone hasn't died. Your houses, gardens, and the foundations of your learning institutions are all built upon the bones of humanity. Whether you realize it or not, you've slept over a grave every night of your life."

"A delightful thought." I wondered how I could possibly sleep with Winston Bennet scratching at the lid of his coffin. Then, an even more frightening possibility crossed my mind.

"Kara? Will your crystals lose their charge?"

She laughed again and it irritated me, which she seemed to sense.

"I'm sorry. Please forgive me. Tell me, where did you find the crystals?"

"In a nearby cave."

"How long do you suppose they've been there?"

I shrugged. "I don't know for sure, hundreds of years, I guess. I don't think

B.K. Crawford

anyone knew about the crystal cave until Daddy and me found it a few weeks ago."

Kara nodded. "Yes. There are nearly thirty-thousand years between us, J.J. If the crystals haven't lost their charge in all that time, are they likely to die anytime soon?"

No wonder she'd laughed at me.

"What about you?" I ventured. "Don't you need to sleep?"

She didn't scoff this time, but I knew I'd asked a stupid question the minute it left my lips.

She offered me a sad smile and answered, "I am no longer a physical being."

Right.

In the end, we decided it best to separate the crystals, leaving only the beetle's violet glow as a protective night light. I hoped it would be enough to keep the bugs at bay. Using my lumpy field bag for a pillow, I stretched out on the cold floor. Four hundred ugly spiders jumped side-by-side with the sheep I counted before I fell asleep.

I awoke with a gnawing hunger. Rifling through the field bag, I pulled out the bologna sandwich I'd prepared the night before and tore into it with gusto, washing it down with juice. Only after I'd satisfied my hunger did I wish I hadn't eaten the sandwich all at once. I had no idea how long I might remain trapped inside the tomb.

Convinced I did myself no service by worrying about food, I moved the beetle closer to the crypt door and spent an hour or so searching for a way out. Not surprisingly, I found no exit mechanism on the door, no handle, no keyhole—nothing at all. If anyone has ever been buried alive in a mausoleum it's not likely they walked away, not with doors designed like the inside of a refrigerator.

In frustration, I grabbed the crowbar I'd left on the top of Winston's pedestal and slammed it into the door, pounding and screaming until my bones could take no more. Hands numb, I dropped the crowbar and glared at the stubborn door.

The dog whined. I thought it strange and oddly sweet the mutt had lingered. Crawling to the door, I pressed my cheek to the frigid stone and called out, "Go get help." In response, I heard nails scraping against stone and realized the noise that had frightened me the previous night was the dog trying to dig its way in. If I couldn't dig out with a crowbar, the dog couldn't hope to dig in.

B.K. Crawford

But, what if someone saw the mutt acting strangely? Maybe they would wonder about it and come to investigate.

"Good dog," I yelled. "Good, good dog."

With nothing to do but hope the dog might attract attention, I assembled Kara's crystals and watched them do their magic.

"Did you sleep well?" She asked.

Staring at her, I didn't answer. I might ask some stupid questions now and again, but so did she.

"Hello," I said. "I wondered..." Not quite sure how to phrase the question, I stammered.

"What is it?"

"How, exactly, does your hologram work?"

"Crystals have memory," she began, eager to answer. "They can hold information for millions of years if the stones remain intact. It's simply a matter of programming the stones, or infusing them with essence and memory. As I explained when you and I first met, infusion is accomplished mainly by focus and intent. These techniques are an ancient art, passed down from generation to generation, so they vary from one culture to another, but each method seems as effective as the next. Once the crystals are infused

B.K. Crawford

with information, a light source is required to activate them. That's why each of my crystals emits its own light. Together, they create a pure light, which is used to read the hologram programmed within, as you have seen."

Although I didn't understand the entirety of it, I nodded. Kara must have sensed my lack as she continued, "Do you have recording technology in your time?"

"We have record players."

"What are they?"

I stopped to consider the best way to explain them. "The records are flat vinyl discs etched with grooves. You put them on a turntable that makes the record spin round and round at a specific, constant speed. There's a mechanical arm with a small diamond attached to it that settles into the grooves. As the record spins, the connection between the vinyl and the diamond tip creates sound. Not pictures, just sound. Music, mostly."

"Very interesting," Kara exclaimed. "You must know diamonds are a hard crystal? But, imagine people thirty-thousand years from now uncovering one of your vinyl records. Without the mechanical arm needed to play

B.K. Crawford

the record, they might assume your disc is some sort of pottery, dinner plates perhaps. Similarly, my crystals, if separated, become nothing more than pretty stones. The lights they emit enable them to communicate with one another."

"I've heard their chirping. But, the reason I asked is, can the light of your hologram expand far enough to see outside the crypt?"

Surprised, she raised an eyebrow. "Yes. If you wish. The light can extend one-hundred feet, or so. In this case, it's far enough to see outside."

"Can you go see if anyone is out there?"

"Of course."

I watched the light expand off the crystals until Kara's image disappeared through the crypt roof. A minute or two later, the light retracted and she returned.

"There's no one out there, but a dog is sleeping outside the door. Based on the position of the sun, I would say it's mid-morning."

"Thank you." I felt relieved to know I had a companion with very useful skills.

A few hours passed uneventfully, except for a great deal of stomach grumbling. Kara and I spent most of the time trying to

B.K. Crawford

concoct a scheme to help me get out of the crypt, none of it worth the thread it would take to sew a pocket on a piss ant's jeans.

By early evening, the knots in my stomach had tightened and all I could think about was food. I rummaged through my field bag for the umpteenth time, knowing I hadn't left a morsel in there. I sipped juice—at least it had sugar—but the canteen had grown light as well with only a few ounces left.

"Play a game with me," Kara prodded.

I rubbed my abdomen, trying to soothe the riot.

"Tell me about your favorite food."

I looked at her like she'd gone mad.

"Pineapple is mine. We make sweet cakes with it. My mother has invented a thousand pineapple recipes because she knows how much I love it."

My stomach grumbled.

"You're not helping," I complained.

"Tell me about your favorite food."

I told her Daddy makes world-famous cheeseburgers.

"Imagine holding one in your hand. Feel the weight of it. Then, take a big bite and let it swirl around your mouth. Chew slowly and focus on the taste."

B.K. Crawford

"You're nuts."

She laughed. "Honestly, I'm trying to help. Just try. Close your eyes. Smell the burger."

Why not? I thought. It's not like my stomach could growl any louder. Besides, I could smell the burger already.

I closed my eyes and saw myself standing next to Daddy at the grill. Smoke rose off the burner and into my nostrils, delivering the heavenly scent of seared beef. Fat popped and crackled as it cooked, spitting now and then. The heat of the grill warmed my face as I drew closer, watching gobs of grease drip over the sides and through the grates. Daddy flipped the burger and reached for the cheese. He says the secret is in the cheese. He slapped a slice on the burger, letting it melt completely, and put a second slice on top of the first, allowing it to melt only slightly, then threw the burger on a toasted bun and handed it to me. I parked a pickle in the middle, doused it with ketchup to overflowing, and bit into it. The first bite always seems the best as the cheese sticks to my teeth and the juice fills my mouth, coating my tongue, the ketchup adding a tart chaser. Doing as Kara suggested, I took my

B.K. Crawford

time eating the burger, delighting in every bite. When I finished, I licked my fingers.

To my surprise, my stomach had quieted down and I felt much better. Not for one minute did I think that little trick would work forever—at some point, I would need real food—but it worked this time and for that, I felt grateful.

I sent Kara out to scout the cemetery several times, hoping she might see someone passing by, but with no success. It would seem cemeteries aren't very popular places. When she came back saying it had grown dark outside, I released a deep sigh. I'd spent twenty-four hours trapped inside.

Mirroring the ritual of the night before, I separated Kara's crystals and lay down on the cold marble floor, where I shivered until sleep took me.

When I woke up, I tried to swallow, but a fiery sensation in my throat made me wonder how in the world I might've swallowed a mound of fire ants that seemed as angry at having been swallowed as I was in hosting them. My throat burned like a stretch of desert sand and a nagging itch persisted.

B.K. Crawford

Familiar with the pain, I suspected tonsillitis as I'd suffered through the ailment twice before when Momma treated me with hot tea and ice cream while I took pills the doctor prescribed. I had none of those things with me and no way to get to them.

No matter how hard I tried, I couldn't escape the tomb, but trouble had waltzed in during the night without the slightest hindrance.

I reached for my canteen. Almost empty. Forcing myself to swallow past the pain, I took three short sips, hoping to wash away the discomfort. Unfortunately, it only made things worse. Testing my forehead, I felt the burn of a high fever. Sleeping on the cold marble must have been too much for my system; that and eating air burgers for dinner.

The thought I'd resisted since becoming entombed broke through my defenses: *I'm going to die here.*

"Oh no," Kara said when she appeared, "You're ill."

I squeezed my throat, swallowed hard, and nodded. My body's desire for water stood front and center in my thoughts, like a spoiled brat demanding candy *now*.

B.K. Crawford

"You must fight the illness." Kara's expression was filled with concern.

"I don't have any water," I moaned, "and nothing to eat."

"Use your mind. Pray, meditate, imagine yourself well."

In my mind, I heard Daddy tell the cop lady, It ain't Sunday,' and I sighed.

"My grandmother, Miss Tilly, says strict religion causes a rift between us and God. She says it's better to have a personal relationship no one can touch."

Kara smiled. "I like your grandmother. But, you need to believe you can heal. Prayer and meditation can give that to you. In my land, we believe the power of the mind is greater than material things. Healing begins by guiding the mind."

Hunger and thirst jabbed at me like the tip of a sharp sword, giving birth to a sarcastic tone, "Like eating imaginary food?"

"But, it helped."

I gave her a weak nod, conceding the point.

"Do you use candles in your society?"

"Sometimes, but, mostly light bulbs."

"What energy fuels your light bulbs?"

"Electricity."

B.K. Crawford

She indicated she understood with a curt nod. "Is there a difference between candle light and electric light?"

I thought about it for a minute.

"Candle light isn't as bright and it varies depending on the height of the wick and air conditions. Light bulbs provide a more consistent light."

Excited, Kara responded, "Exactly. Now imagine your mind as a light source. When attempting to perform a specific task, the use of a candle-like energy may cause you to stumble because the energy varies, whereas, a more coherent light, like a laser beam will ensure precise execution of the task. When people meditate, they organize the energy of the mind and focus it like a laser, granting them faster and more precise results."

Raising my eyebrows, I stared at her. "You sound like my science teacher, Mr. Reick."

"Meditation will help you heal."

I'd eaten an imaginary burger and still woke up starving and sick to boot. I felt my fury rise.

"I want food and water. I want out of this hell hole. I want to go *home*," I shouted, grabbing my throat when the outburst caused the pain to intensify.

B.K. Crawford

Just then, I heard whimpering outside the tomb and turned toward the door, shocked. The dog hadn't left. Didn't it need food and water, too? Why did it linger? For me?

Slipping down the wall, I slunk to the floor. Poor, pitiful, ungrateful me. I got myself into this mess and I could have been stuck in the crypt alone, but I had Kara. What's more, it seemed she would do everything in her power to help and I repaid her generosity with snippy comments and unrestrained outrage.

"I'm sorry," I whispered. "I'm afraid. Plus, I don't know how to meditate."

"It's alright," Kara cooed, "I'll help. Start by telling me about your favorite place."

I didn't even have to think about it. The little creek behind our house has always been my special spot.

I told Kara about the way the mermaid moss sticks to the rocks under the water, the tadpoles playing there, the dragonflies, the way the wind whispers through the trees, the birds breaking out in song, the twinkling sunlight dancing on the water, the cool rush as the water kisses my toes, and how I go there when I'm troubled.

B.K. Crawford

"So, you find it easier to think when you're there?" She asked.

"Always."

"You know how to meditate, J.J. That's what you're doing when you sit beside your creek."

"Really?"

"I'd say you're quite skilled. You can use the creek to help you heal. Please go, sit beside the water and see yourself vibrant and healthy."

Happy to leave the dreary tomb—if only in my mind—I took Kara's suggestion and spent an hour at the creek. I don't know if it helped much, but I did find the experience a sweet escape.

A rumbling stomach jarred me from my fantasy and I found myself searching the corners of the tomb for signs of life. Gagging, I realized I might be hungry enough to eat anything that moved. In an effort to take my mind off the stomach pangs, I asked Kara a question I'd wanted to ask since we first met.

"How did you die?"

She flinched and I immediately felt guilty for asking such an insensitive question.

Composing herself, she answered, "If someone paints a portrait of you when

B.K. Crawford

you're ten years old, that picture holds the essence of who you are and what you know up to the age of ten, but it says nothing about the kind of woman you will become. My hologram cannot know anything of my fate beyond the age of fourteen because that's when I created it."

"How could you live so long ago and still seem as much alive as I am?" I said in frustration.

"The hologram technology we use has its limitations. It cannot record the future, as I've just said. However, consciousness never dies, it's eternal. Because some of my consciousness is present in the infused hologram, you and I can interact with one another."

"You're like a genie in a bottle." I was still in awe, and I knew, if she could, Kara would grant my every wish. Sadly, most of the backwoods folks I know would likely attempt to destroy Kara's crystals out of fear; a fear I readily understood as I hadn't forgotten how her hologram nearly scared the bejeebies out of me when I first saw it and how Bo reacted fearfully as well.

"What's it like where you live?" I asked.

B.K. Crawford

Kara told me many ordinary things about her life, which seemed very much like mine. She collected pretty rocks, and had box after box of them stored under her bed, just like me. We both enjoyed exploring our environment, we liked to read, and we sometimes allowed our curiosity to get the best of us.

I especially agreed her with her when she quipped, "Adults forget the magic surrounding them and instead of enjoying the beauty of the world, they war in greed, struggling for power and control." Elaborating, she told me a division had arisen between the spiritual and material sects of her society and that this division had begun to erode the civilization from the core. That, she said, was why she and others had saved their consciousness in crystals and left them in safe places, "Usually in caves, far underground, or off planet."

When I asked why they had done so, she said they wanted to warn people in the future of the dangers of making the same mistakes.

I asked what she meant when she said they had taken their crystals off planet.

B.K. Crawford

   "We developed interplanetary travel long ago with the help of a star federation out of Andromeda. Alien influence has always existed in Atland. Our ancient histories document visits from many alien species. In fact, they are credited with the creation of the human race as many of them are masters of genetic manipulation. Some species came to offer technology and others to offer wisdom. There are also those who are devout materialists who came to the planet for gold. These also siphon energy, which they use to cloak themselves as humans. These materialists attempt to present themselves as gods but many in Atland are not fooled. They are slave masters with no real empathy for humanity, though they attempt to create the illusion. The energy they derive from fear acts like an addictive drug, with which they are always intoxicated. Their influence, I fear, may one day bring Atland to her knees."

   Thoughts of complete disbelief rushed into my mind, but ultimately, I had to admit to the hours I'd spent engrossed in the story of the flying saucer crash at Roswell, New Mexico, in 1947 and my personal feelings that the

B.K. Crawford

government had orchestrated a cover-up surrounding the incident.

I thought about the tables filled with human skeletons in various sizes and shapes located at the bottom of the shaft at my dig site. Genetic manipulation?

I recalled snippets of a speech John F. Kennedy made a couple years ago about secret societies. He'd said a secret society exists that would try to expand its "fear of influence." Did the president of the United States know about the aliens Kara told me about? And, if he did, did he have a plan to do something about them?

I also couldn't shake the comment Mrs. Dunaway had made about the gods, and my own experience of watching the orb steal Bo from the ground right before my very own eyes.

"I don't think those nasty aliens have left the planet yet," I exclaimed. I told her what Mrs. Dunaway said about her son being robbed of his eyes and his soul. Then I told her what happened to me and Bo the other night when the orb chased us down.

"It sounds like the war continues," Kara said.

"War?"

B.K. Crawford

"Nothing on Earth is more valuable than living energy and no energy is more pure than that of an innocent child. The materialists feed on fear and pure energy. Sacrificial ceremonies involving innocent children are considered a feast among them. But they have always had opposition. I would guess the alien race that abducted you and your friend had no evil intent, or..."

"Or, I wouldn't be alive to tell about it."

Kara nodded.

I began to wonder if Hank Hornbrook belonged to those evil aliens, sucking on souls so he could pretend to be human. But then I wondered why he didn't kill Bo at the carnival and why he didn't use his opportunity to kill me here in the cemetery. True, he did expect me to die at his hand, but he could have killed me in an instant. For some reason, he didn't. Had he told the truth when he said he never killed any of those kids? Prior to finding me inside his house, his efforts seemed geared toward warning me to stay away. Miss Tilly said Hank worked as a government aide. Was he someone else's flunky?

B.K. Crawford

All at once, it seemed too much to think about.

The space around me began to spin. I suddenly felt as though I'd jumped from an airplane without a parachute—no ground beneath my feet, nothing to grasp to slow my hellish descent, a hammering thrum beating inside my skull. Collapsing to the floor, I fought for air, gulping, unable to satisfy the abrupt need.

Kara's urgent cries stirred me, "J.J., *wake up*."

I rubbed my throbbing head. "What happened?"

Eyes wide, she gasped, "You fainted. I thought," she stuttered, "I thought you were..."

"Me too." I clutched my throat. Swollen and inflamed, I could barely swallow. Hot to the touch, my skin raged with fever and my tongue felt like sandpaper grating against my teeth. I needed something to drink. Propping myself against a nearby wall, I opened my canteen and swallowed the last ounce of juice, gagging as I forced it down.

I heard the vague tones of Kara's voice— blurry words spoken, or whispered, as if off in the distance, so far away I couldn't make out

B.K. Crawford

what she said. I began to shiver
uncontrollably, my stomach turning
cartwheels, my head swimming, a dark cloud
covering my eyes like a blanket, taking Kara's
light away.

"I can't stay," I whispered and faded into
oblivion.

I heard a mournful weeping. Did someone
die?

Pressing on the cold stone beneath my
chest, I raised my head, slightly, off the floor.
When the tomb came into view, I searched
for Kara's face, but she had extended her
light through the roof of the crypt to go
scouting. When she returned, I saw a stream
of tears washing over her cheeks and I
wished I could give her a hug.

"You're alive," she blurted. "There's
someone in the cemetery. A woman. She
saw me."

"Am I still dreaming?"

"*No.* You've been unconscious for hours. I
heard people singing, so I stretched out for a
look. It's dark outside and I saw a woman
kneeling over a nearby tombstone. I begged
her for help. She looked up, called me
Mother Mary, then ran back into the church.

B.K. Crawford

There are people in there tonight. Get up, make some noise."

Determined to get to my feet, I pushed with all my might, but my head slammed back into the cold floor where the pain held me down. I simply didn't have an ounce of strength left.

"I'm sorry," I whimpered.

Kara wailed, "If you die, I swear I'll be the first to meet you, but please don't do it now, we're so close. Your time isn't over yet. Can you hear me? J.J.?"

I smelled a strange perfume. Lilac? Sweet and purple. A slight pressure glanced over my brow accompanied by a warm sensation. Strong arms lifted me to a sitting position and held me there, while someone else put a cup to my lips. *Water.* I drank and sputtered, leaning in for more.

"You poor dear," I heard a woman gush. "An angel watches over you."

"Collect her things," an elderly gentleman instructed, "We'll get her out into the air where she can breathe."

"The stones," I pointed, "break them apart, give them to me."

B.K. Crawford

Several men from the church service helped put me in the backseat of a car owned by the sweet old couple who had forced the crypt doors open and discovered me there. They told me the entire neighborhood had been searching all weekend and exclaimed it a miracle to find me inside a crypt where no one would have thought to look if the Lord's angel hadn't stood guard over my soul.

Momma and Daddy looked giddy with relief when the car pulled in front of the house and beeped the horn. Daddy came tearing across the lawn in his bare feet and carried me straight to bed while Momma got on the phone to call for a doctor. Grateful to be alive and at home in my own bed, I thanked God for Kara.

I'd survived two nights sleeping with the dead, but I had some explaining to do.

B.K. Crawford

I Confess
ВЖВ

Daddy grounded me, but only until I'm eighty-five.

It took four days for my throat to begin to feel normal again. In that time, I confessed everything to Daddy and introduced him to Kara. When he first saw her face appear, I could see a wild desire in his eyes, the desire to blast her to smithereens with his shotgun. But, once I convinced him to calm down, they began speaking to one another and became fast friends. As I watched them talk, I saw in my father a small boy, full of life and wonder. I realized, then, where I got my thirst for adventure.

Kara taught me how to use the light of the blue ankh to help hasten my healing. I simply placed the stone over my throat and allowed the crystal energy to work its magic. By the end of the week, I felt the itch to get out of bed, but Momma insisted I continue to rest. At least she had finally allowed visitors to come by.

I sat next to Bo on my bunk bed, recalling my time in the crypt.

B.K. Crawford

"It's an awful curse," he chuckled, "being you."

"After everything we've been through," I lamented, "We still don't know who killed those kids."

Bo raised an eyebrow. "I'm pretty sure we do. We just don't want to admit it."

We heard a voice we immediately recognized coming from downstairs. The lady cop had come to talk to Momma and Daddy. Bo and I crept down the stairwell and perched there, ears pressed to the wall.

"A trafficking ring," the Lieutenant asserted. "The Feds found overwhelming evidence at Forest Ledge Academy. Some of the boys were beaten to death by clients who tasked Hank Hornbrook with the disposal of the bodies. He sank most of them in the swamp near his house, but it seems he saved a few corpses for his own twisted pleasure, dressing them up in costumes, exacting some sort of revenge against his mother. We're continuing the investigation and we expect you to keep your daughter out of the way."

Momma showed the Lieutenant to the door and the cop lady left in her black Buick. Bo and I returned to my room.

B.K. Crawford

"Have you ever heard a thicker line of bullshit in your entire life?" I seethed.

A few hours later, Daddy called us to come outside. I enjoyed my first rays of sun in over a week while we sat at the picnic table, watching Daddy grill his famous burgers. When we finished eating, Momma cleared the table and went inside to clean up.

Bo and I sat in uncomfortable silence while Daddy glared at us. When he finally spoke, he leaned across the table to say, "Trafficking usually involves girls, not boys."

That's exactly what I thought when I heard the cop lady spout her line of crap.

"After what Mrs. Dunaway told me about the gods, it seems closer to the truth those kids were tortured in sacrificial ceremonies," I said.

Daddy nodded in agreement. "Only someone high up on the pole could weave such a ridiculous story and expect us to buy it."

Bo chimed in, "I bet the Newhouse family didn't report Davey missing because Mr. Newhouse knows some of the higher ups aren't your garden variety humans. The families of the victims probably kept their

B.K. Crawford

mouths shut to protect remaining family members."

He was likely right.

"Maybe the president has secret plans to fight them," I added, hopeful.

Daddy leaned back, crossed his arms over his chest, spit into the grass and mumbled, "How do you fight the gods?"

Sealing The Dig
ВЖВ

A week later, I picked up the ringing phone and heard Bo's excited voice, "Read the paper." Setting the phone down, I searched until I found the paper in Daddy's recliner and unfolded it. I scanned the front page but didn't see anything of interest. Picking the phone back up, I squawked, "What am I looking for?"

"Page seven."

I flipped the pages. On page seven, the paper had printed a tiny article claiming Hank Hornbrook had hanged himself. Dropping the paper to the floor, I immediately wondered why Daddy hadn't said anything. Did he not see the article? Or...did Daddy give old Hank a hand in meeting his maker?

I never asked.

By the end of the summer, the government had sealed off the dig site on Briarhill. Seems they had someone watching my every move and their greasy spy had followed me to the site and alerted the Feds to the presence of my dig. Furious, I raged and grumbled for days. Daddy did his best to keep me calm while we commiserated

B.K. Crawford

together, both of us knowing we couldn't do a darn thing about it.

Then, a woman we'd never seen before stopped by the house one day in a muddy Jeep. Tall, thin, blonde, and rugged looking, she smiled and jumped out of the vehicle, heading across the lawn like she'd known the Houston family from the beginning of time. As she approached, I noticed she wore a field bag over her shoulder.

Waving, she called, "Hello."

She said her name was Carola Bourne, an archeologist out of State University. Reaching to shake Daddy's hand, she kept her focus on me and didn't seem to notice much when Daddy refused to return her courtesy. Right away, I noticed she wore one of the official identification badges from my site. She had some nerve showing up on our doorstep. I felt my cheeks burn and I could barely hold my tongue. Taking Daddy aside, she spoke with him for a few minutes, then he nodded and left her alone with me.

"I have something for you." She reached into her field bag and pulled out an identification badge with my name on it. How gracious of the Feds to allow me access

B.K. Crawford

to my own dig. I made no move to indicate I would accept her gift.

Her smile grew wider. "We have a lot in common, J.J.," she said. Reaching into her bag once more, she withdrew a small stone and showed it to me. She held a perfectly shaped crystal in her hand, a Siamese cat. "It has a yellow glow," she chuckled. "I found it inside a large cave in South America." Leaning closer, she practically whispered, "It has a brother and a sister."

Mouth gaping, I stared at her. She *knew*.

"Take the badge," she coaxed. "No one should have the right to take over someone else's find. Your dig should remain yours." She handed me the badge and, this time, I took it.

"Word of warning, though. Don't go to the site alone. They're on to you, Miss Houston."

B.K. Crawford

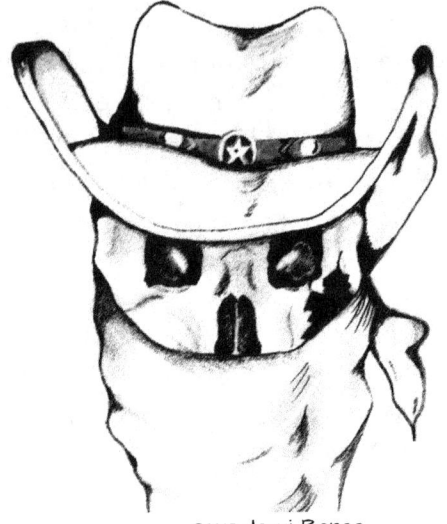

©2015-Jaqui Renee

www.facebook.com/authorBKCrawford

B.K. Crawford

A Note From The Author

Thank you for taking this journey with J.J., I appreciate your time. I hope you've enjoyed the adventure and will join me for others. As any Indie author, I rely on my readers to help spread the word. And so, I ask a favor of you... Please take a moment to leave a review on Amazon to help others know which books will suit their reading tastes. Your review is important in helping to get the word out. If you feel inspired to recommend this book, I thank you from the depths of my heart and remain forever in your debt.

What a hoot!

Ever Yours, ~B.K. Crawford~

B.K. Crawford

More Titles by B.K. Crawford

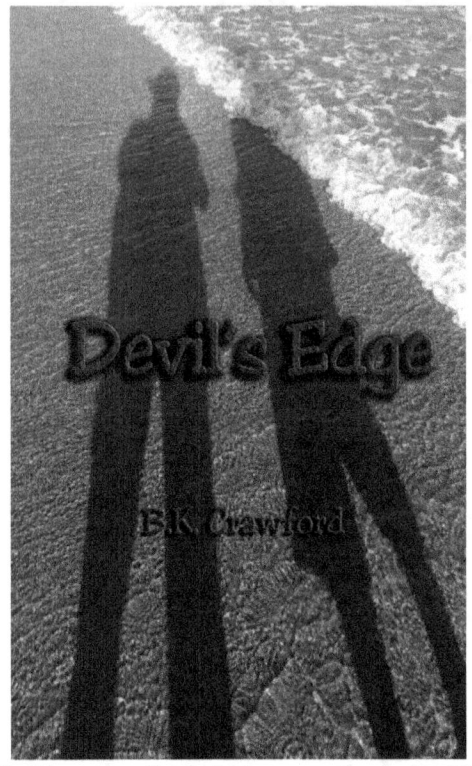

Devil's Edge, a small tourist town on the coast of North
Carolina, hasn't known much by way of skullduggery
and murder since Blackbeard bit into his last
doubloon, but the past is about to come screaming
back with a hair-raising vengeance.

B.K. Crawford

Fantasy fans will flip over this rowdy satire featuring the skillful
and mischievous sorcerer, Merlin the Great.

Farrin Lockwood will one day become the Queen of Collingswood,
but not if she doesn't master patience first. Hoping to outwit a
menacing sorcerer, she must face the white dragon, rescue her best
friend from an unthinkable marriage, enlist the help of a shape-
shifter, and team up with the infamous Merlin, who will attempt to
prepare her for battle against the bloodthirsty Morgana le Fay.

B.K. Crawford

B.K. Crawford

www.ingramcontent.com/pod-product-compliance
Lightning Source LLC
Chambersburg PA
CBHW061325170626
46817CB00001B/323